THE PLAIN PRAIRIE PRINCESS

Crossway Books Youth Series by Stephen Bly

THE NATHAN T. RIGGINS WESTERN ADVENTURE SERIES
The Dog Who Would Not Smile
Coyote True
You Can Always Trust a Spotted Horse
The Last Stubborn Buffalo in Nevada
Never Dance with a Bobcat
Hawks Don't Say Good-bye

THE LEWIS AND CLARK SQUAD ADVENTURE SERIES
Intrigue at the Rafter B Ranch
The Secret of the Old Rifle
Treachery at the River Canyon
Revenge on Eagle Island
Danger at Deception Pass
Hazards of the Half-Court Press

RETTA BARRE'S OREGON TRAIL SERIES
The Lost Wagon Train
The Buffalo's Last Stand
The Plain Prairie Princess

~ Retta Barre's Oregon Trail ~

BOOK THREE

THE PLAIN PRAIRIE PRINCESS

STEPHEN BLY

CROSSWAY BOOKS

A DIVISION OF
GOOD NEWS PUBLISHERS
WHEATON, ILLINOIS

The Plain Prairie Princess

Copyright © 2002 by Stephen Bly

Published by Crossway Books

        a division of Good News Publishers

        1300 Crescent Street

        Wheaton, Illinois 60187

Cover design: David LaPlaca

Cover illustrator: Bill Dodge

First printing 2002

Printed in the United States of America

Library of Congress Cataloging-in-Publication Data

Bly, Stephen A., 1944 -

   The plain prairie princess / Stephen Bly.

     p.   cm. — (Retta Barre's Oregon Trail ; Book 3)

   Summary: In 1852 on the Oregon Trail, twelve-year-old Retta keeps her family safe from prairie raiders and a band of Sioux as they spend a few days away from the wagon train during her mother's illness.

   ISBN 1-58134-393-0 (TPB : alk. paper)

   1. Oregon National Historic Trail—Juvenile fiction. [1. Oregon National Historic Trail—Fiction. 2. Overland journeys to the Pacific—Fiction. 3. Frontier and pioneer life—West (U.S.)—Fiction. 4. Indians of North America—Fiction. 5. West (U.S.)—Fiction.] I. Title. II. Series.

PZ7.B6275 Pl   2002

[Fic]—dc21   2001007099

                                            CIP

15	14	13	12	11	10	09	08	07	06	05	04	03	02
15	14	13	12	11	10	9	8	7	6	5	4	3	2	1

For
Amanda Carter

Have I not commanded you?
Be strong and courageous.
Do not be frightened, and do not be dismayed,
for the LORD your God
is with you wherever you go.

JOSHUA 1:9 ESV

One

A long the North Platte River, three days west of Robidoux's Trading Post near Scotts Bluff, Wednesday, June 29, 1852

> *Dear Diary,*
> *I think that someday when I look back on this journey, meeting Dance-with-the-Sun will be the most important event, but everyone here is more excited because I killed the poor, old buffalo. I didn't really kill him, but a girl gets a certain reputation, and they all believe it to be true.*
>
> *Coretta Emily Barre, 12½*

For over an hour a steady line of spectators with lanterns hiked out to gawk at "Retta's buffalo." Ben Weaver and Travis Lott acted as tour guides while Retta and the girls stayed with Gilson and Mrs. O'Day until they talked things through. Retta left mother and daughter embracing with tears and resolving to keep trying and keep praying.

When she returned to her own wagon, Retta was surprised to find William, Andrew, and Lerryn perched on boxes and crates around a small fire. A lamp burned inside the wagon where she could hear muted voices.

"What're you all doing out here? What's going on in there?"

"Where have you been, li'l sis?" Andrew asked.

"Eh . . . at the Gilsons' wagon. I told William and Lerryn I'd be there."

Andrew held his hat in his hand and rolled the brown felt brim. "I went to find you, and you weren't there. The wagon was empty."

"We . . ." Smoke from the smoldering fire engulfed Retta. She coughed before she finished the sentence. ". . . we had to go out on the prairie and look for Gilson."

Lerryn tugged on the lace cuffs of her dress sleeves. "It would have been a good time to stick around the wagon instead of playin' hide-and-seek. Or was it a scavenger hunt?"

"You sent me off. Besides, I wasn't playing. Gilson needed help, and then there was this buffalo . . . What do you mean, a good time to be here? What's going on?"

William pulled off his spectacles and rubbed the bridge of his nose. "Mama had a bad spell."

"She's bleedin'," Andrew murmured.

Retta felt as if someone had kicked her in the stomach. "Oh no . . ." She burst into sobs.

William strode to her side and put huge, strong arms around her shoulders. "It's okay, Coretta. She'll be okay. Mama's stronger than you think."

Retta dried her eyes on her dress sleeve. *Lord, next to Papa, William has the nicest hug in the world.* "Who's in there with her?"

Lerryn brushed the corners of her eyes with her fingertips. "Papa and Mrs. Weaver. Christen's mom has had experience with this sort of thing, you know."

Retta stared at the tall shadow cast on the inside of the white canvas wagon tarp. "Is there anything I can do?"

Andrew stretched his long legs out in front of him, his

boots only inches from the smoking fire. "Papa said for all of us to wait out here."

"And pray," William added.

"Lord Jesus, this is Coretta Emily Barre . . . and Lerryn and Andrew and William. Our mama's in there sick, and we want her well. And we can't do anything about it without Your help. So. . . well, You can do it. I guess that's about it. Bye. In Jesus' name, amen."

She lifted her head.

William was grinning at her. He gave her another hug and dropped his arm to his side. "I didn't mean that you had to pray right this minute."

"Oh . . ." Retta puffed out her cheeks. "Can I go up and see Mama?" she finally blurted out.

William squatted down next to the fire and poked the coals. "Papa said for us to stay out here. He needs to talk to us."

Retta moved over in front of her sister. "Everything will be all right, won't it?"

She noticed Lerryn trembling. Then tears trickled down from her eyes.

Retta glanced around at her brothers. "What is it? What's happening?"

Andrew hugged Lerryn as she dropped her head on her brother's shoulder and broke out sobbing.

Retta felt tears rolling down her own cheeks. "I'm crying, and I don't even know why. What is it? Please tell me."

William slipped his hand in hers and walked her out in the darkness away from the wagon. "Let's go where no one can hear us."

Retta tried to wipe her cheeks, but she couldn't stop crying. "William, I'm really, really scared."

"We all are, Coretta. Listen, Lerryn was with Mama when she had that spell and started bleeding. Mama had a lot of pain and said some things she didn't mean. Lerryn took it hard."

"What did she say?"

William took a deep breath. "This is tough on me too, little sis."

"Please, I want to know what you all know."

"Mama was hurtin' bad . . . and she said . . ."

He paused, and Retta put her head on her brother's chest. He put his arm around her shoulders.

"She said she didn't know why the Lord didn't take her home because she couldn't go on livin' with such pain. She . . . darlin', she asked Lerryn to pray that the Lord would take her to heaven."

"And Lerryn couldn't do it?"

William held her fingers tight. "Of course not. Could you?"

Retta puffed out her cheeks and shook her head. "No . . . never."

"Mama begged her. When Lerryn refused, Mama told her that she was a rebellious and uncaring daughter."

Retta couldn't hold back the sobs. Her knees were weak.

He pulled out his bandanna, wiped his eyes, and then patted her face with it. "She didn't mean it. We all know that. It was the pain talkin'."

"But why does Mama have to have such pain? She's such a quiet, gentle, sweet lady. Everyone says so."

"I know, Retta. I know. I guess we just have to trust the Lord in this."

"Poor Lerryn. No wonder she feels so bad. I should have been there with her."

"You want to go back now?"

Her voice was soft, yet firm. "Yes, I do."

When they had trudged back to the Barre wagon, Andrew and Lerryn were still standing arm in arm.

Retta cut in and slipped her arms around her sister. They were almost the same height. Lerryn clutched her tight. Retta laid her cheek against her sister's. *Lord, never in my life has Lerryn needed to hug me. But now it's like we've hugged all our life. Maybe we have . . . in a different way.*

All four Barre children were still huddled next to the fire when Mrs. Weaver crawled down out of the wagon. "My goodness, it looks like a stump revival meeting out here."

"How's Mama, Mrs. Weaver?" William asked.

Mrs. Weaver fastened the top button of her high-collared black dress. "She should be fine now for the night."

Andrew stepped over to her and lowered his voice. "How about tomorrow and the next day?"

"One day at a time, Andrew Barre."

"Can we go see her now?" Retta asked.

"Your papa said he had things to talk to Julia about. Then he wanted to talk to you all together. Give them a little more time by themselves."

Retta clutched Mrs. Weaver's arm. "Mama's going to live through this, isn't she?"

Mrs. Weaver shoved blonde bangs back and rubbed her forehead. She patted Retta's hand. "Now, Coretta dear, we're all in the Lord's hands. No one has any guarantees. I've never known any woman who trusted the Lord more than your mama. So I reckon you can trust Him with her. Tell your papa that Mr. Weaver will be waitin' up to talk to him whenever he wants to."

"What about?" Retta asked.

Mrs. Weaver strode off into the darkness, but her words floated back. "Your papa will tell you."

William stooped down and stirred the fire. "We might as well sit down and wait."

Lerryn and Retta sat arm in arm on the trunk.

"You know what's funny?" William said. "In the past couple months the four of us haven't sat still in one place more than three or four times. We're always busy going somewhere else. Yet here we are, all sitting around the campfire."

"Do you ever wish we were back in Ohio?" Retta asked.

"Oh, yes, sometimes," Lerryn replied. "Especially when I think about our house and my room."

"And our barn," William added.

Retta laid her head on her sister's shoulder. "Do you ever think about the lane down to the river?"

Lerryn leaned her head against Retta's hair. "Sure. Remember how sweet it smelled when the trees were in bloom?"

"Well, I'm glad we're here," Andrew blurted out. "We prayed about it all winter. Remember, every mornin', day after day after day? It seemed like the right thing to do, and so we did it."

Lerryn sat up. "You're glad we're here even though Mama's so sick?"

"We have no guarantee Mama wouldn't be sick at home," Andrew replied.

Retta sided with Lerryn. "But at least she'd be in her own house with a real roof over her head and Dr. Ossimo living just down the road."

William kicked at the fire. "If you think it's tough on us, think what it must be for Papa."

"Have you noticed how he's aged on this trip?" Lerryn pointed out.

"We've all aged." William rubbed the light brown stubble on his square chin. "Why, look at Coretta Emily. She looks about twelve years old."

"I am twelve," Retta declared.

A wide grin broke across her oldest brother's face. "See?" he laughed.

At the sound of boots pounding toward them, all four stared west until Bobcat Bouchet came into view.

"Missy, I'm glad to see you up. Your Indian is up at Colonel Graves's wagon wantin' to talk to you."

"Two Bears?" Retta stood and braced herself on William's shoulder. "I . . . I need to stay here. Mama's sick, and Papa said to wait here."

"You can go on, little sis. We'll all be here," William assured her.

"No, I'm not leaving Mama. I'm not going to be left out."

"I'll go with you." Lerryn stood beside her. "I haven't met your Indian yet."

Retta looked over at her sister's bright blue eyes. "Really?" *Lord, it's the first time in five years that my sister has wanted to do something with me, and I just can't go.* "I can't leave Mama. I'm just too scared of missing something again. What does Two Bears want?"

Bouchet reached down and brushed biscuit crumbs off his brown leather vest. "He wants to talk to you about your buffalo."

"I figured all that wagon-train talk was just another wild Retta Barre story," William mumbled.

"Little Sis has a buffalo?" Andrew asked.

Bouchet nodded. "A dead one. Rumor is, she killed it with her coup stick."

Lerryn brushed her blonde hair back. "Her what?"

"You know, my rock hammer that Dance-with-the-Sun gave me."

Lerryn's mouth dropped open. "Who?"

"I told you all about it."

"You mean it was all true?"

"Yes. Mr. Bouchet, can Two Bears come see me here? Tell him my mama is sick, and I can't leave her. I think he'll understand. It won't be the first time he has come to our wagon."

They all stared at Retta.

"Well, really, just once before."

"I'll tell him, Missy." Bouchet hesitated in the shadows. "Tell your mama I'm prayin' for her, too."

"Are you a prayin' man, Mr. Bouchet?" Lerryn asked.

"I reckon if the good Lord ever had a healin' touch for anyone, it would certainly be for someone as kind as your mama," he replied.

"The Lord bless you, Mr. Bouchet," Retta said.

"Well, Missy . . ." The scout coughed and then continued, "I reckon He'll do just that since you asked Him." Bouchet slipped into the black night, only his boot heels revealing his direction.

Retta had just finished telling her sister and brothers about the ordeal of looking for Gilson O'Day and about the wounded buffalo that followed her when a dark-skinned, barefoot man in buckskin trousers, white cotton shirt, and a red bandanna around his forehead appeared behind their wagon.

"Is that your Indian?" Lerryn asked.

Retta jumped up, scurried over to Two Bears, squatted down on her haunches, and drew in the dirt. Two Bears did the same.

"Who are the others?" he asked.

"You know my brother William. He helped us look for Ansley and Shy Bear. The younger one is my other brother Andrew. The girl is my sister Lerryn."

He studied the three who sat next to the fire staring back at him and Retta.

"The girl does not look like you." Two Bears's voice was low, showing no emotion.

Retta drew a sun in the packed mud at her feet. "No, Lerryn looks a lot like our mother."

"That is too bad for her." Two Bears traced a moon next to Retta's sun.

"Too bad for her?" Retta formed stars in the mud sky. "Lerryn is the pretty one."

"You are mistaken." Two Bears drew a coyote head howling at the moon. "You are the one who looks Shoshone. There is no higher compliment than that."

"Thank you very much."

"You are welcome. Your sister merely looks like Missouri."

"We're from Ohio," Retta corrected.

"You see, Missouri, Ohio—they all look the same. Rather pale and weak, if you ask me. I am sorry your mother is sick. My mother died from smallpox that she contracted when washing clothes at Fort Bridger. I know what it is like to have a mother sick."

Retta started to puff out her cheeks, but pressed them in with her fingers. "We're waiting for my father to come out and tell us how she is. That's why I couldn't leave. What can I do for you?"

He leaned forward until his nose was only a couple of inches from hers. "I hear you killed a buffalo."

"Oh, he had been shot. I think he was dead before I accidentally hammered him."

"Do you know who shot him?" Two Bears asked.

"No."

"Did you see the buffalo alive?" he probed.

"Oh yes. He followed me across the prairie."

"And you were the last to strike him with a weapon?"

"Yes, but it was an accident. I was just trying to help my friend Gilson get up. The coup stick bonked him on the nose."

"It is his misfortune. The buffalo is yours," Two Bears declared.

Retta glanced over her shoulder to see her brothers and sister straining to hear every word. "It is?" she replied.

"That is the rule of the prairie. The final blow that kills the animal signifies the owner of the animal. Would you like to trade for him?"

"You want a dead buffalo?"

"Of course. There is much meat for my family. Do you want to trade?"

"Yes . . . eh, no!"

Two Bears pulled back. "No?"

"I don't want to trade. I want to give him to you."

Two Bears nodded. "Yes, and I will give you something in return."

When Retta shook her head, her bangs bounced from side to side on her forehead. "No, you don't have to do that. You're my friend, Two Bears. Can't Red Bear give her friend a gift?"

"Yes, most certainly."

"Good. That's settled."

"And Two Bears will send his friend Red Bear a gift."

"But you don't need to do that."

The Indian folded his arms across his chest. "You mean, it is allowable for you to give a gift, but I may not give you one?"

Retta glanced back at her brothers and sister. Then she turned back. "You're allowed to give any gift you like."

"Thank you."

"You're welcome."

Two Bears raised up, and Retta stood with him.

"Are you going to take the buffalo in the morning?" she asked.

Two Bears rubbed his chin. "No, we will butcher him now."

Retta glanced across the pitch-black prairie. "Tonight?"

A slight grin penetrated his leather-tough face. "Yes. Would you like to help?"

"Eh . . ." Retta puffed out her cheeks.

"No, you need to stay with your mother. I remember. Good night, Red Bear."

"Good night, Two Bears."

He walked over to the fire. "I am sorry that you are sick."

"Oh, I'm not sick," Lerryn explained. "It's our mother."

"Yes, I know." He ambled straight out into the dark night.

"I can't believe this," Lerryn said.

Retta walked back over to them. "What?"

"You were talking to a real Indian."

"You can't believe that there was a real Indian on the prairie?"

Lerryn shook her head. "I can't believe my little sister is friends with a real Indian."

"He's very nice, you know."

William poked at the fire. "I can't believe how well li'l sis talks to them. You look so relaxed, like you've done this all your life."

"Two Bears is very easy to talk to. I wasn't this friendly with Dance-with-the-Sun, and Tall Owl scared me to death."

"How many Indians do you know?" Lerryn asked.

"I don't know. When I wear my buckskin dress, they seem to welcome me right in," Retta said. "Some of them say that I look sort of Shoshone. I don't think so. I don't look like anyone."

"I'll tell you what I can't believe," Andrew hooted.

"That's the first time I ever heard anyone say it's too bad Lerryn doesn't look like Coretta."

Retta's face flushed. "That was rather silly for him to say, wasn't it?"

"Not for me," Lerryn replied. "He thought I look sickly. It just reminded me that we are only as attractive as the one looking at us thinks we are."

Retta bit her lip. "He didn't mean it as an insult."

"Coretta Emily, never in my life did I want to look like an Indian, until about ten minutes ago. But then I realized that you and I are different, and that's okay. So you get to be princess of the Shoshone—if you'll let me be queen of the wagon train."

Retta laughed. "Oh, I'll let you. But Ansley might not."

The four sat around the fire for several moments, not saying anything.

Retta leaned forward with her elbows on her knees, her chin on her hands. *Lord, we've been living in this little wagon for seven weeks, and yet we're seldom together. Just the four of us—the Barre children. I'm very happy and scared to death at the same time. I don't know what Papa wants to tell us. I don't know why he and Mama keep talking. It can't be good news. But I don't know what news it could be. Lord, I'll ride with Mama every day and cook and clean and wash and sew. She doesn't have to do anything. Lord, my papa says I have strong bones for a girl. Now I know he tells me that so that I won't think I'm fat, but he could be right. I am strong, and I can work hard.*

Retta watched William fuss with the fire. Andrew had his arms folded across his chest. Lerryn kept rubbing her hands as if to dry them off.

Lord, I do like my sister. Sometimes we don't get along, but I like her. She's like Mama, but younger and snotty. Well, sometimes.

Two

*A*ndrew and Lerryn sat back to back, leaning against each other for support. Retta stretched out across the trunk, her head on William's lap. His hand stroked her thick, unruly hair. She drifted in and out of sleep. She thought she heard a coyote. Or maybe she dreamed about a coyote. Or perhaps it was a Cheyenne signal.

Lord, sometimes I like being the youngest. This is one of those times. They all take care of me.

I like the freedom to be me . . . and yet the comfort of knowing they're watching out for me.

I dread the day they get married. Maybe soon.

William will belong to Amy Lynch.

Lerryn will look after Brian Suetter.

And Andrew? Well, Andrew may never make up his mind, even though there's always a long line of girls interested in him. Perhaps he'll be around a long time.

Someday it will be just me and Mama and Papa.

I hope I'm not too lonesome.

It could be worse.

Lots worse.

It could be just me and Papa.

Lord, I'm really, really scared.

William rubbed her cheek with his palm. "Here comes Papa."

She sat straight up and strained to adjust her eyes to the dark night. No lanterns were lit, and only the stars shone into their camp.

"Papa, how's Mama?" Retta blurted out.

"Darlin', that's what I need to talk to you all about. I'm sorry to keep you up so late. I didn't want to come out here until your mama went back to sleep."

"Is she resting now?"

"She's exhausted. She's asleep."

"What're we going to do, Papa?" Lerryn asked.

"Your mama and I talked it over for a long, long time. Some things are not easy for me to talk about. I want you all to know that the biggest mistake I ever made in my life was bringin' your sweet mama out on this prairie this year. I should have listened to her. I should have waited until next year. I let the Donation Land Act sucker me into thinkin' we had to go claim that land now. My reckless impatience is inexcusable. I will live with this the rest of my life. No matter what happens, I want you to know that this was your papa's folly, and he knows it."

"What do you mean, 'no matter what happens'? What's going to happen?" William asked.

"I don't rightly know all that will happen, but it's important to me to tell you that I can be a stubborn, even prideful man. So I want you to know that I take full responsibility for this."

"For what, Papa? Mama was sickly before we left Ohio," Andrew pointed out.

"Which is precisely why I should have stayed in the states. However, we are here . . . on the prairie . . . almost halfway to Oregon."

"So what do we do now?" Lerryn pressed.

"We make the best decisions we can from this point forward. Your mama's sick, real sick."

"But she's going to be all right, isn't she, Papa?" Retta asked.

Retta studied his square-jawed silhouette against the white canvas wagon top.

"Darlin', we're all in the Lord's hands, and ever'one of us has to trust Him for the future. Same is true for Mama. We're just trustin' Him day by day. But one thing we know, she can't travel for a day or two. Every bounce of that wagon brings pain and danger."

"What're we going to do, Papa?" Retta pressed.

"We aren't goin' to move the wagon. We'll park it and rest up a few days."

"We're goin' to hold up the wagon train?" William asked.

"No. I wouldn't do that if I could. No one wagon has the right to stall the others. I sent word to Colonel Graves to pull out in the mornin' and leave our wagon."

Lerryn clutched her hands together and bit her knuckles. "They're going to leave us?"

Mr. Barre paced around the campfire. "They lost a couple days in the storm and another today pulling the California-bound out of the bog. They have to keep up. The worst part of the trip is up ahead."

Andrew unfastened the buttons on his shirtsleeves and began to roll them up. "Are we goin' to go on our own, Papa?"

"Only for a few days. As soon as your mama is better, we'll either catch up or lag back and join the wagon train behind us."

"You mean, we'll just be sitting out here in the prairie by ourselves?" Lerryn asked.

"I'll make some arrangements at daylight." His voice was almost a whisper.

Retta leaned forward. "What kind of arrangements?"

"Your mama and I talked it through. We decided that we should send you four on ahead without us."

William jumped to his feet. "Send us where?"

"Now hear me out. The only way I could convince your mama to sit out her bad spell was to promise I'd send you children with the wagon train. So I'll put William with Colonel Graves. He needs your help. You're the best man with the horses in this whole outfit."

"Second best next to you, Papa," Retta corrected.

"Don't interrupt, darlin'. Andrew, you'll probably go with Sven Neilsen. He needs help, and you've been wantin' to ask him about gunsmithin'. Should be very educational. We'd like Lerryn to travel with Mrs. Ferdinand. You know that she's been lonely ever since we buried her husband back at the bluffs. And, li'l darlin', you'll be with the Weavers, of course. They've been your second home ever since you were a little penny. Mrs. Weaver said it will be fine."

William folded his arms across his muscled chest. "You can't split us up, Papa!"

Mr. Barre sighed. "Well, son, I can't ask anyone to take all four of you. That's just too big a burden."

Andrew stood three inches taller than his older brother. "That's not what William meant. He meant that you can't ask us to go off and leave you and Mama."

Mr. Barre's voice softened. "It's just for a few days."

Lerryn scooted up next to Andrew. "Papa, it doesn't matter how many days. We aren't doing it."

"You don't understand. The decision has been made. Your mama and I have talked this through."

Retta moved up next to William. "But, Papa, you didn't talk to us."

"You're only eleven. I don't have to—"

"I'm twelve, Papa, but I won't go off and leave you and Mama."

Mr. Barre put his hands on his hips. "I don't reckon I have to consult you on everything."

"I'm twenty years old, Papa, and this is something you do have to talk to me about. I'm not going," William announced.

"Neither am I," Andrew added.

"I've struggled, cried, and prayed about this all evening. Don't grieve me by disobeying me."

"Don't ask us to do something our hearts won't let us do," Lerryn pleaded.

Mr. Barre paced in front of them. "Now look. You don't understand. This is a very serious situation . . ."

"We understand, Papa," Retta insisted.

"No, I don't think you do."

"Papa, we know that Mama is very sick," William said, "so sick she could die. So sick she wants to die. And she just might die."

"And we know you can't move her," Andrew added.

Lerryn slipped her arm into her father's arm. "We also know that a wagon stuck on the prairie by itself is a target for Indians and raiders. We know that staying back will mean danger to all of us."

Retta stepped up and grabbed his other arm. "But to go off and leave you and Mama would doom our entire lives to misery and regret. Papa, we know what we're getting into. We're not little children."

He hugged his daughters. "Do you mean to tell me that you'll disobey my direct orders?"

"Papa, we're begging you not to order us," Lerryn implored.

"And if I do order you?"

"May the Lord have mercy on us," William replied. "And you'll have to decide whether it's best for us to follow you or to follow the Lord's leading."

Retta laid her head on her father's strong shoulder. "We won't go, Papa."

"We're the Barre family. We don't split up," Andrew declared.

Retta felt his shoulder start to shake. "You aren't making it easy for me," he finally choked out.

"Is it easy to send us away, Papa?" Retta asked. She could see the tears roll down her father's face.

"No, darlin', this is the toughest day in my entire life." He brushed his eyes with his shirtsleeve. "You four do understand what I'm saying, don't you?"

"You're saying we could die right out here on the prairie all alone," William said.

"That's what I'm saying."

"Papa," Retta said, "I don't want to live without you and Mama and William and Andrew and Lerryn."

"Well now, darlin', we don't know what the Lord's future plan for our family looks like."

"We know He planned for us to be together. And if we are to be split apart, let's let Him do it, not us," William asserted.

"That's your decision?" Mr. Barre said.

"Yes, sir, it is," Andrew affirmed.

"Do you know that you are all as stubborn as your mama?"

"Yes, sir, we do know that," Andrew replied.

Mr. Barre walked over to the wagon and tapped on the box. "Did you hear all that, Julia?"

Her voice was very weak but decisive. "Yes, I did."

"Then we're all stayin'."

"Yes, I reckon we are," she replied.

After the children had greeted their mother from the back of the wagon, Mr. Barre lined them up next to the dying fire. "Now I need you all to get some sleep. Even though we aren't pullin' out in the mornin', there are some things we need to do."

"You want us girls to sleep under the wagon with William and Andrew?" Retta asked.

"No . . . well . . . maybe just tonight, but after that I'll want you girls in the wagon with Mama every night."

"What do we do in the mornin', Papa?" Lerryn quizzed. "Do we just sit here and wait for them all to leave?"

"More or less. I'm not movin' that wagon one foot until your mama gets better. So at first light you boys cut out our horses, cows, and oxen. Push them out on the prairie to the south and hold them until the others are driven out of sight. I'll come out and spell you. When everyone is gone, we'll drive them up here to the wagon."

"We could make a rope corral for them," William suggested.

"Yep, we just might have to do that."

"How about us?" Lerryn asked.

"Li'l sis can build the fire, like always. Big sis, do you want to cook or sit with Mama?"

"I want to cook."

"You do?" he asked.

Lerryn's voice was almost a whisper. "I think Mama might want someone else to look at."

"She didn't mean those things, darlin'."

"I know, Papa." Lerryn rested her chin on her chest. "But even when you fall down by accident, it still hurts."

Mr. Barre stared at Lerryn for a moment.

His voice was low.

And soft.

"You're right, sis." He turned to Retta. "So, darlin', when I tap, you crawl up in the wagon to be with Mama. I'll start a fire."

"I can start the fire, Papa. That's my job," Retta insisted. "Then I'll crawl up in the wagon with Mama. Let me start the fire."

He shook his head. A slight smile dawned on his rugged face. "Did I ever tell you I have the best family in the world?"

"Oh, Papa" Retta scolded, "you tell us that all the time."

They rolled the big canvas awning out on the ground under the covered wagon, and Mr. Barre tossed down the quilts. All four stretched out with their clothes on. The girls removed their shoes and stockings. Andrew stretched out at the east end. Next to him was Lerryn, then Retta, then William. Their heads aimed toward the river, and their feet pointed to the prairie.

"Are you scared, William?" Retta whispered.

"About sleeping under the wagon?"

"No, about being left out here on the prairie by ourselves."

"Just a little maybe. I'd be a lot more nervous without all of you around."

"You mean without Papa?" Retta pressed. *When William talks softly, he sounds just like Papa.*

"No, I mean all of us," he replied. "Somehow family makes it better."

"Do you think Indians will come attack us, Retta?" Lerryn asked.

Retta turned toward her sister. "You're asking me?"

"You know more about Indians than the rest of us combined," Andrew stated.

"I know the Shoshone won't attack. They're my friends, and they're in a hurry to get to Fort Bridger. And I know the Cheyenne that are led by Dance-with-the-Sun won't attack. At least, as long as I wear my buckskin and carry that coup stick. I think they just wanted the Arapaho."

"What about that mean Indian?" Lerryn asked.

"If Tall Owl gets free, he's liable to be mad at you," William said.

"He's by himself," Retta reasoned. "If he broke free, he would have to take us all on."

"If he gets free from that bunch, it means he has helpers. Remember how they dragged him across the river?" William reminded her.

"I don't want to think about it." Retta shuddered. "Let's think about good things."

"Like what?" Lerryn questioned.

"Like Oregon," Retta whispered. "William, what're you looking forward to most about Oregon?"

"Havin' my own farm."

"Are you goin' to file for 320 acres of your own?" Andrew asked.

"Yep."

"You goin' to marry Amy Lynch?" Retta probed.

"If her daddy lets me. He said we couldn't marry until I held that Donation Land Act claim in my hand. Course, if I was married, my wife could get 320 acres, too."

"How about you, Andrew?" Retta asked.

"I'm goin' to start me a blacksmith shop. Papa said if I helped him build a barn, I could use it for blacksmithing until I get a place in town."

"What town?" Lerryn queried. "Did you ever wonder what town we'll be near?"

"Maybe we get to name one," William chuckled. "Did you ever think about that?"

"We could call it Barresville!" Retta ventured.

"We came from Barresville," Lerryn reminded her.

"Well, there can be two of them!"

"We could name it Cutler after Great-grandpa," Andrew suggested.

"We could name it after Papa," Retta offered.

"Eugene? Have you ever heard of a town called Eugene?" William chuckled.

"Well, in that case, I think Rettasburg has a nice ring to it."

"No one asked me what I look forward to in Oregon," Lerryn put in.

"Well?" Andrew pressed.

Lerryn rolled over on her back. "School."

"I don't know if there are any schools in Oregon yet," William mumbled in a sleepy, deep voice.

"Well then," Lerryn maintained, "I'll just start one. I'll be the teacher."

"Really?" Retta rolled over next to her sister.

"Yes, and you have to be one of my pupils."

"Okay, but I get to sit in the back of the class. In Ohio they made me sit up front."

"I wonder why?" Andrew jibed.

"Very well, you may sit in the back. As long as you behave yourself and don't write notes to the boys on your slate."

"Yes, ma'am," Retta giggled.

"How about you, little sis?" Andrew probed. "What do you look forward to in Oregon?"

Retta wrinkled her nose. "Wood for fires instead of chips. Do you know how disgusting it is to have to collect buffalo dung every day?"

"No, really," Andrew pressed. "What're you looking forward to?"

"Having my own horse. I'll have enough money saved up to buy a horse by the time we get to Oregon. In fact, I hope to have one by Independence Rock."

"I think . . . we should all . . . go to sleep," William mumbled.

Retta scooted down under the quilt. Lerryn scrunched in beside her. Their faces almost touched.

"Retta," she whispered.

"Yes?"

"Do you have your coup stick?"

"It's over here between me and William."

"Can we put it right between us?"

"Why?"

"For protection. I'd feel safer."

"Sure."

Retta tucked the stone hammer near their shoulders. She felt Lerryn's arm drape over her back. Retta looped her arm around her sister's neck.

"I'm glad you're my sister, Retta."

She could feel her sister's warm breath. "I'm glad you're my sister too, Lerryn."

"I'm scared, Retta."

"I know. So am I."

"Which scares you most—being left on the prairie or Mama takin' sick?" Lerryn asked.

"Mama's sickness."

"Yeah, me too. Retta, no matter what happens, we'll still take care of each other, won't we?"

Retta hugged her sister. "Yep."

"Are you really only twelve?"

"You know I am. Why did you ask that?"

Lerryn rubbed her shoulder against Retta's. "Tonight it seems like you're much older."

"Well, if I wet the quilt, you won't think that," Retta snickered.

Lerryn scooted away a little but kept her arm on Retta's shoulder.

Three

Christen Weaver and Joslyn Jouppi huddled by Retta's side just as daylight finally broke across the prairie. The wagons cast long shadows to the west under scattered clouds in the sky. A busy hum of conversation, shouts, and laughter mingled as all the wagons lined up. Crates, boxes, and pot hooks were stored and children accounted for.

Odors of fried meat and straining oxen drifted across the encampment. Retta knew that at the front of the train, Colonel Graves and a few others would be making final plans. Somewhere toward the front, Taggie Potts's father held a bugle in his hand, waiting for a signal.

Everyone was ready to leave.

All except the Barres.

Retta wore her brown cotton dress with the collar too tight to button. Her forehead was deeply tanned. Unlike Retta, the other girls wore bonnets that matched their dresses.

Joslyn's thin lips quivered. "I can't believe this. Two days ago I was crying because I had to go on without you. Now I'm doin' it all over again. This isn't fun, Retta. I'm tired of having to say good-bye."

Retta felt the dry west wind chapping her lips. "I know, Joslyn, but it's only for a day or two."

"It doesn't feel like just a day or two."

"What's it feel like?"

Joslyn took Retta's hand. "Like I'll never see you again."

"When Mama feels better, Papa said we could catch up."

Christen seized her other hand. "My mama wanted us to stay with you, but Daddy said . . ." She paused and took a deep breath. "Oh, you know how daddies are. He said one of our families needed to get to Oregon before those other wagon trains do. He said he'd hold a good home site for your family at gunpoint if he needed to until you catch up."

Retta squeezed both of their hands at the same time. "We'll be back with you in a few days."

Christen's dark brown hair curled out from under her calico bonnet. "In that case, do you want me to keep Ansley away from my brother?"

Retta's smile pushed toward her ears. "How're you going to do that?"

"I thought I'd tie him up and toss him in the canvas sling under the wagon."

"With the buffalo chips?" Retta giggled.

Christen raised her chin and glanced down her nose at the other girls. "Yes. What do you think?"

"And leave him there for three or four days?" Joslyn laughed.

"Yes," Christen laughed. "Until Retta catches up with us."

"But what if that takes two or three weeks?" Joslyn teased.

"In that case, Ansley can have him," Retta proclaimed.

"Speaking of the red-haired queen bee." Joslyn pointed to the girl on horseback galloping straight at them. The rider's straw hat was tied under her chin with a forest-green ribbon.

Ansley reined up, but her long-legged black horse

danced a little sideways. "Retta, I can't believe you're staying back. It's dangerous to go it alone." She jumped down and led her horse up to the girls.

Retta lowered her chin and her voice. "Mama can't be moved."

Ansley stepped up in front of Retta. "Well . . . well . . . we'll miss you."

All three girls stared at Ansley.

Ansley licked her full, dark red lips and took a deep breath. "I'll miss you," she blurted out.

Retta reached out her hand.

Ansley paused and then grabbed it firmly. Her voice softened. "Really, Retta, the wagon train won't be the same without you. Everyone says so."

"Thanks, Ansley. I'm going to miss everyone, too. But we'll catch up in a few days. Mama's bad spells don't usually last too long."

"I'll look in on Gilson every morning and evening. I know she'll miss you terribly."

Retta stared at her. *Lord, I don't think I've ever seen Ansley like this. Is she serious? Is she using me? Why is she being so pleasant and nice?* "Thank you. I would appreciate that."

Ansley stroked her horse's nose. "As soon as she's able, I'll let her ride my horse with me."

"I think she'd like that. It'll give her something to look forward to," Retta said.

"That's very generous, Ansley," Christen affirmed.

"Is that what it's called?" Ansley winked at Retta. "I always wondered what that word meant."

There was an awkward pause. Then Ansley grinned, and all four girls broke into laughter.

Ansley brushed red hair off her ears. "And I might even leave Ben alone if you do a favor for me."

Retta rocked back on her heels. "What do you want me to do?"

"Tell your brother what a wonderful girl I am, how I'm very mature for my age, and—"

"But William already has a girlfriend."

Ansley's green eyes danced. "Not that brother!"

"But Andrew is four years older than you."

"How much older is your papa than your mama?"

"Eh, almost seven years."

"And my daddy's sixteen years older than my mother. So what does age have to do with it?" Ansley argued.

Retta scratched her head and wrinkled her nose. "Okay. I'll tell Andrew you're cute, demure, charming, coy, glamorous, intelligent, and rich."

"Well," Ansley laughed, "you got the first and last ones right. Bye, Retta. I hope you hurry and catch up with us soon."

Ansley reached over and hugged a stunned Retta Barre. Then the redhead climbed on her horse and rode up the row of wagons.

"Is that the same Ansley MacGregor we all know and love?" Retta grinned.

"She surely has changed in just a few days," Joslyn observed. "I wonder what she's scheming?"

"Sounds like she's scheming to catch Retta's brother," Christen replied.

"That's bad news for the rest of us," Joslyn declared. "Don't you dare tell your brother anything about Ansley."

"Why? Are you after my brother, too?"

"Coretta Emily," Christen lectured, "every unmarried girl in this wagon train wants to latch on to your brothers!"

"Really?"

"That's the only reason we hang around you—to be close to your brothers." Joslyn tried to keep a straight face, but she ended up laughing and throwing her arm around Retta.

"And all this time I thought you were my friends because of my sparkling personality."

"Yeah, that too," Christen said.

"We're goin' to miss you bad, Retta, 'cause there's no one on earth who has more fun or gets herself into more adventures than Retta Barre."

"You two have been such great friends. I'll miss you most of all. And now I guess I'll even miss Ansley."

"She's getting so nice we won't even have anyone to talk about," Christen quipped.

"You can talk about me," Retta offered.

Christen folded her arms. "Coretta Emily Barre, everyone in the whole wagon train talks about you already. The first time an Indian party cuts our trail, they'll be saying, "'I wish our little Shoshone princess, Miss Retta, was here. She'd know what to do.'"

"I don't know anything. I just sort of stumble along, and it turns out okay."

Christen turned to Joslyn. "And she's modest, too."

"Are you goin' to wear your buckskin the whole time you're out here?" Joslyn asked.

Retta rubbed her nose with the palm of her hand. "I guess I haven't thought about it."

"You have to promise me you'll wear the buckskin and carry your coup stick everywhere," Christen insisted.

"Oh, I'm goin' to be fine. I've got Papa and my brothers to look after me."

"And they have to look after your sick mama and your sister, too," Joslyn pointed out. "Christen's right. You simply must wear your buckskin."

Their conversation died when Mr. Potts sounded his bugle.

"There's the call to roll out. You two go on. I'll see you in a few days."

Joslyn clung to Retta's arm. "We aren't going to see each other again!"

"We most certainly are."

"I don't want to leave you, Retta." Tears streamed down Christen's face. "I'm really scared for you."

"Go on before I cry." Retta puffed out her cheeks and held her breath.

Joslyn and Christen pulled away.

"You have to promise to wear your buckskin dress," Joslyn called back.

"Every day!" Christen shouted.

"I promise . . ." Retta's voice faded as the wagons began to roll. "I promise . . ."

Like a train leaving a depot, the wagons lumbered out onto the short brown grass of the prairie.

Colonel Graves.

Bobcat Bouchet

The O'Days.

The Landers

The Potts.

The Weavers.

Mrs. Ferdinand.

Old Sven Neilsen.

And all the other wagons and ponies.

Everyone was gone except one lone wagon.

Twelve-and-a-half-year-old Retta sat on a green trunk and watched the entire string of wagons roll over the rise on the prairie. Her father hiked up with his rifle over his shoulder. "Well, li'l sis, I reckon it's just us."

"This place seems even more empty and lonely now, doesn't it?" she asked.

"Well, darlin', I reckon the Lord is just as close to us here as He would be in church in Barresville."

"I know, Papa, but we've been traveling with two hundred people for so long. Now they're gone."

"Think of it as a vacation."

"Are we going to just sit here?"

"I don't want any of us to go far from the wagon today. Mama was in a bad way last night. We'll huddle around. You four set up the awning and make camp permanent."

"And then what?"

"We wait."

"How long, Papa?"

"Until the Lord tells us it's time to move."

Retta thought it was the longest day they had spent since they left Ohio. William and Andrew occupied themselves with the care of the animals. Lerryn and Retta gathered what chips they could find, never getting out of sight of the covered wagon.

Papa stayed in the wagon with Mama.

And Mama slept.

And slept.

And slept.

That night after supper Retta and Lerryn bunked in the wagon. Mr. Barre and the boys camped outside. Retta woke up once in the night when her mother called out for Grandma Carter. Lerryn had said something, and Retta fell back asleep.

At one point Retta thought she heard a rooster's crow at the dawn, but she woke up to the blackness of night. All she heard was a distant coyote and a horsefly buzzing somewhere under the canvas wagon top.

The next day started as the last one ended. Nothing stirred on the prairie except the Barre family.

William and Andrew had a horse race.

William won.

Lerryn and Retta mended several shirts and stockings.

Papa stayed by Mama's side.

And Mama slept.

But she did wake up hungry.

And then she slept some more.

The sun hung three-quarters of the way across the pale prairie sky when her father climbed down out of the wagon. His cotton shirt was sweat-stained, and he carried his rifle and shot case. His powder horn hung at his side. "What're you doing, darlin'?" he asked Retta.

"Just listening, Papa."

"What're you listenin' to?"

"My heart, I guess. There isn't any other noise."

"And what is your heart sayin'?"

"It's saying that I want Mama to get well so bad I hurt all over."

"I know, darlin'. That's just how I feel. She's eatin' today, and that's good. The Lord's been good to us. It's been a nice, quiet day. Sometimes no sounds are better than too many. There are no Indian war chants, no thunderin' buffalo stampede."

"And no other wagon train catching up with us. I'm kind of surprised about that, Papa."

"Maybe they got off the trail."

"Maybe *we* did."

Mr. Barre rubbed his chin. "You could be more right than you know, darlin'. Either way, here we are."

"What're you goin' to do now, Papa?"

"Thought I'd hike over to the river and hunt a little.

Maybe we can eat somethin' that isn't pickled or salted. Your mama is gettin' tired of preserved meat."

"Are you going by yourself?"

"The boys are busy. I'll just be gone a short while."

"Can I go with you?"

"No, you stay here in case big sis needs you for something."

"Papa, can I wear my buckskin dress?"

"Sure, darlin', you wear whatever you want. You goin' to change in the middle of the day?"

"My buckskin doesn't show dirt like this cotton one." Retta shaded her eyes as the sun broke out from under a small, round, puffy cloud. "It's a purdy day, Papa."

"It surely is, darlin'. I'll be back in a few minutes. We'll cook up somethin' special for supper."

Retta crawled up into the wagon. Lerryn sat on a pillow on top of the green trunk, talking with Mrs. Barre, who wore her flannel nightgown.

"Hi, Mama. I didn't know you were awake."

"Baby, I can't sleep all the time." Her mother reached over and patted Lerryn's hand. "I understand we're all alone out here."

Retta bit her lip. "All the other wagons are gone, Mama."

Mrs. Barre's voice was very soft. "I know, baby. Are you scared?"

"Not as much as I thought I would be. I think I'm a little lonely for my friends. That's okay, isn't it?"

"We all miss our friends."

Retta studied her mother's pale face. Each word seemed to be delivered in pain. "I can look for miles and see no one," Retta continued. "Being in the wagon train is like living in a portable town that packs up and moves every day. It's like living in town. Now it's like we moved to the country—

only we didn't move. Town packed up and moved away from us."

Mrs. Barre raised her hands to her temples. "Where's Papa?" she asked.

"He went to the river to hunt." Retta smiled. "You want me to go fetch him?"

"No . . . no . . . I guessed that's where he went. I made the mistake of mentioning that I didn't think I could eat any more salted pork." She paused for a moment and then held her chest and took a deep breath. Retta could see pain shoot across her mother's face. "I should have known he would go hunting. Did he take William and Andrew?"

"Oh, no, Mama, he went by himself. The boys are with the animals in the tall grass. Do you want me to go get them for you?"

"He shouldn't have gone by himself," Mrs. Barre replied, her jaw locked, her eyes glazed.

"He won't be gone very long," Retta soothed.

"He knows better than to go off and leave us," Mrs. Barre snapped, still staring at the white canvas of the wagon top.

"Mama, it's okay. Daddy can take care of himself," Retta assured her.

"Well, he needs to take care of a lot more than himself."

Lerryn reached over and tried to smooth the wrinkles from her mother's brow. "Mama, you know how Papa likes to please you."

Mrs. Barre lay back down on the pillow and stretched her arm over her eyes. "He had no business leaving us out here by ourselves—just three women."

That's the first time Mama ever said I was a woman. "Andrew and William are here with us," Retta reminded her.

"They're just boys!"

Lerryn took her mother's hand. "Mama, William is going to be twenty-one."

"Whose side are you on?" Mrs. Barre demanded.

Retta looked at her sister. Lerryn shook her head and then stroked her mother's cheek. "Mama, are you hurting bad again?"

"Why are you changing the subject?"

"Because I want to take good care of you, and if you're hurting, maybe there's something I can do."

Mrs. Barre managed a raspy whisper. "The pain I have never goes away, never dulls, never relents. It just numbs the mind and crushes the spirit."

"Let me roll you on your side, Mama, and I'll rub your back," Lerryn offered.

"Thanks, darling, that would be wonderful. You take such good care of me."

Lerryn turned to Retta and mouthed the words, *"It's all right now."*

"I'm going to wear my buckskins," Retta announced.

Lerryn massaged Mrs. Barre's back as Retta changed her clothes at the other end of the wagon. She pulled on the dress, smoothed it down, tugged on the moccasins, and then laced and tied them. She wiggled her toes against the smooth, soft leather.

She pulled the headband out of her valise and tied it around her forehead. The eagle feather swooped down across her left ear. She had just stood up, clutching her coup stick, when Mrs. Barre rolled over on her back.

With her chin tucked to her chest, Retta asked, "How do I look, Mama?"

"That's a very nice costume, darlin'. Now you go on out and play with the other girls."

Lerryn laid a finger over her mouth as a signal for Retta not to reply.

"Okay, Mama." Retta glanced at her sister. "I'll be right outside if you need anything," she whispered.

A cool easterly wind whipped the tent flap as she climbed down. The dirt around the wagon was hard-packed and dry but not yet dusty. To the south of the wagon the wind pressed the brown buffalo grass flat. Retta stared out toward the animals. Andrew and William stood outside the rope corral, holding their horses.

She hiked out toward them.

"Li'l sis, you're a purdy sight to see comin' through the prairie grass all decked out like an Indian," William remarked.

"I feel like a little girl playing dress-up. Do you think I should put it away?"

"Nope. Coretta Emily, I suppose we all have to grow up fast enough. Enjoy bein' twelve," Andrew replied. "Seein' you all suited up like that makes me smile."

"And we surely need some smiles. How's Mama?" William asked.

Retta dropped her head. "She's still hurtin' bad and sort of . . . says things she doesn't mean or even remember saying."

"She didn't get mad at big sis again, did she?" William asked.

"No. She did get mad at Papa."

Andrew rubbed dirt off his neck with a big red bandanna. "Why?"

"Well, she mentioned she wanted to taste something besides salted meat, and he went down to the river to hunt. Now she's mad at him for going alone."

"That ain't Mama talkin'. She knows he can take care of himself," William said.

Retta swung the coup stick back and forth by the wrist

strap. "That's what I told her. She said that he's forsaken us out here."

Andrew stared back at the covered wagon. "Hard to imagine Mama in that much pain."

"I surely wish the Lord would answer our prayers." She strolled over to the rope corral and surveyed the animals. "Did you know that Mrs. O'Day said she quit praying for Gilson because it didn't do any good? I don't think she should stop praying, do you?"

"To stop prayin' is to stop talkin' to the Lord. I don't reckon that ever helped anyone," William offered.

"It helped me when I stopped prayin' for Rachel Lamont." Andrew grinned.

"How did that help?" Retta asked.

Andrew laughed. "That's when I met Laura Beth."

Retta punched him in the arm. "Are you thinkin' about Ohio?"

"I guess so. I don't know why. Ohio is gone forever."

"We won't ever go back, will we?" she stated.

"Not until they get a railroad all the way to the Pacific," William said.

"You think that will happen?"

"I hope it don't happen soon. I kind of like the land empty," William remarked.

"We lathered up our horses racin'. So we're goin' to take them over to the river to water 'em before evenin' and then picket them close to the wagon. We can look for Papa while we're down there," Andrew offered.

William stepped up by her side. "You want one of us to stay here, li'l sis?"

Retta stared around the empty prairie. "There's no one out here but us. Go on; we'll be fine. The sooner Papa comes back, the sooner Mama can relax."

"If Mama takes a bad spell, fire the shotgun. We'll be here in ninety seconds," William assured her.

"Where's the shotgun?" she asked.

"Last time I saw it, it was down there by Grandma Carter's cedar chest."

"Will the oxen and cows be all right?" she asked.

"Yep. At least until they get thirsty," Andrew replied.

"How about Papa's horse?"

William glanced over at the dun gelding. "He'll want to follow these two, I reckon. He doesn't mix too good with the oxen and cows."

"I can tether him to a wagon wheel. Can I brush him down?" she quizzed.

William grinned. "You're goin' to spoil ol' Prince."

"I have lots of time."

William and Andrew pulled themselves up into their saddles. "Okay, li'l sis, you can pretend he's your Indian pony."

"Can I draw war stripes on him?" she laughed.

"No," Andrew hooted. "And you can't make him into a chestnut and white pinto either!" He kicked his heels in the horse's flanks, and both brothers raced toward the river.

Four

Retta led the tall dun gelding back to the wagon. Lerryn poked her head out the yellow flap at the back. "Are they goin' to get Papa?"

"They're goin' to water the horses and then look for him. Is Mama still awake?"

"No. She went to sleep. Are you goin' with them?" Lerryn asked.

"No. They just thought Prince would be more peaceful away from the oxen and cows." Retta tied the horse to a wagon wheel. "Lerryn, is Mama still bleeding?"

"She wouldn't let me check. She said Papa could do it when he got back."

"Are you doin' okay, sis?"

"Yeah, thanks. It really seems strange to peek out and not see any other wagons. And to see an Indian princess who looks very much like my sister."

"Do you think this makes me look too much like a little girl?"

"Coretta Emily, that outfit makes you look as old as me."

"Really?"

"Yes."

"Lerryn, that's about the nicest thing you ever said to

me in my life." Retta curtseyed. "Thank you, Miss Barre. That's very kind of you."

"I'll try not to do it too often," Lerryn laughed. "What's happened to us, li'l sis?"

Retta leaned against the wagon tailgate. "What do you mean?"

Lerryn tossed her head, and her blonde hair flopped from side to side. "For ten years we've been at each other most of the time. Then all at once . . ." She snapped her fingers. ". . . you seem like an important friend to me. Did you notice that?"

"Yes, I did," Retta acknowledged. "It really hit home when . . ."

"Everyone drove off and left us?"

"It's down to just you and me."

"That's what was strange for me," Lerryn added. "Everyone left—even Brian—and it didn't bother me nearly as much as the thought of the four of us being split up."

"That would be intolerable, wouldn't it?"

"Retta, I'm glad you're my sister. I like it that you're different from me."

"We certainly look different right now, I reckon. But to tell you the truth, if one has to look like an Indian princess and one like a wagon train queen, I wouldn't mind being the queen." Retta grinned.

Retta brushed Prince's head, shoulders, withers, and back, and then started on his sides and legs. His left rear hoof was lifted up slightly. She knew he was dozing. She was grooming his mane when she noticed his ears perk up. His head turned east.

"What is it, boy? Do you hear something?"

Retta looked eastward but saw nothing.

"Is Papa coming back with the boys?"

The horse continued to stare at the horizon until the top of a wood-paneled wagon came into view, still a mile off.

"Lerryn!" Retta called out.

Her sister poked her head out. "What is it?"

Retta pointed. "Look, we have company."

"Is it the next wagon train?"

"It's only one wagon. I don't even see any outriders."

"You think it's some of those prairie pirates that Colonel Graves warned us about?" Lerryn asked.

"I guess we'll find out."

"What shall we do, Retta?"

"Get the shotgun and stay in the wagon with Mama. William said that if we need them in a hurry, we should fire the shotgun."

"You want me to shoot it?"

"Not until we find out who they are."

"Are we goin' to let them ride right up here?"

"Nope. I'll go out and talk to them."

"Really?"

"Get the shotgun and watch me. Don't fire unless you think you must," Retta instructed.

"Do you know what you're doing, li'l sis?"

"I guess so. I've been playing this part for days."

Retta retied Prince to the wagon wheel and swapped the horse brush for the coup stick. She tramped straight toward the rattling, squeaking wagon.

A man with a thick, dark beard rode on the wheel mule. He carried a rifle across his lap. On the wagon seat sat two more men, both with unshaven faces hidden under wide felt hat brims. The side of the paneled wagon was faded, but the name "Missouri River Mill & Grinding" could still be read.

They kept coming toward Retta. When she got halfway

between the covered wagon and the paneled wagon, she squatted down and started scratching out a large pine tree in the prairie dirt.

The paneled wagon pulled up about fifty feet from her. One of the men on the wagon seat roared, "What's that squaw want, Elmo?"

The man riding the driving mule replied, "Wants to palaver, I reckon."

"Who's goin' to talk to her?" This voice sounded higher than the other two, but Retta didn't look up.

"I don't know no Injun talk. You go on out there, Davy," Elmo hollered.

"Why don't we just swing past 'em and trail the wagon train?" Davy suggested.

"'Cause there's a horse and cows, and there're supplies in that wagon. These Indians must have raided it."

"I can tell you one thing." The third man cleared his throat. "This squaw ain't alone. So watch yourself."

"You really want me to go out there?"

"Davy, you told us you could talk to the Indians."

"What am I supposed to say?"

"Tell her she's a good-lookin' squaw, and you want to marry her," Elmo replied.

"What?"

"The point is, she won't understand nothin'. But maybe you can find out how many of them there are and where the men are. There's only one horse that I can see."

The man in the gray long-sleeved shirt and greasy striped trousers climbed down. He pushed his hat back and moseyed her way. Retta didn't look up but continued to draw.

"Woman, I reckon I need to talk to your husband."

"She looks young, Davy," Elmo shouted. "Maybe she don't have a husband."

"All these heathen get married young," Davy snorted. "Woman, I said, where is your man? Do you hear me?"

Retta continued to draw.

"You got to squat to talk to them, Davy," the third man called out.

"What do you mean, I got to squat?"

"They don't talk unless you squat down there with them," Elmo instructed.

"If you know so much, why don't you come talk to her?"

"'Cause I'm the only one who has bullets left for his gun. I need to keep a good view of the prairie."

"They don't know I don't have any bullets."

"Squat down, Davy!" Elmo screamed.

Davy squatted on his haunches across from Retta.

She glanced up at him without showing any emotion, never looking in his eyes.

"Shoot, she's a young one all right," Davy shouted back.

"Don't you go to smooth-talkin' her," Elmo instructed. "Find out where the men are."

Davy cleared his throat. "You got a . . . a husband around here, ma'am?"

"I thought you knew how to speak Indian!" the third man yelled from the wagon.

"I forgot some words," Davy shouted back. Then he turned back to Retta. "Where's your husband?"

Retta held up three fingers.

"Shoot, Elmo, she's got three husbands!"

"Or her husband is three miles away."

"Indians don't know miles."

"Well, maybe he's three days away. If he's three days away, she just might be lonely." He reached over and touched his grimy fingers to her chin.

Retta swung the coup stick and crashed the fist-sized rock into the man's toe.

Davy leaped up, grabbed his foot, and hopped across the prairie. "She done busted my toe! Shoot her!"

"I'm not wastin' one of our last bullets," Elmo replied. "You were the one stupid enough to touch that savage. You're lucky she didn't stick a knife in you."

Davy limped back to the wagon. "Well, I ain't goin' to do no more negotiations. I say we just pick us out a nice cow for supper and drive on off. I reckon if we drive through the night, we can catch up with that wagon train. Pickin's will be better there."

"Ain't we goin' to look in this here wagon?" the third man called out.

"Nope!" Elmo declared from the back of the mule.

"You ain't afraid of that squaw with a rock hammer are you?" the third man replied.

"Nope, but I do have respect for that shotgun that's aimed out the back wagon flap," Elmo remarked. "Let's jist ride on around them."

"I'm goin' to cut me out a cow," Davy fumed.

"Then do it on foot 'cause I ain't bailin' you out. If we use up our last bullets here, we don't have any left for tomorrow. Next folks we rob have to have lead and a bullet mold, or we're in big trouble."

"She purt near broke my toe!"

"Well, that's why they call them savages. You heard what happened to Moss Starkey."

The wagon rattled north of the Barre covered wagon and kept going west. Retta waited until it disappeared over the rise and then sauntered back to the wagon.

Holding the shotgun, Lerryn stuck her head out. "I can't believe you clobbered that guy in the toe and got away with it. I thought I'd have to shoot him for sure."

"I can't believe I didn't clobber him in the head," Retta mumbled. "What a jerk."

The voice from inside the wagon was weak. "Shoot what, darlin'?"

Lerryn stuck her head back inside. "Shoot a . . . eh, prairie pest, Mama."

"A coyote?"

Retta climbed up and stuck her head inside the wagon. "More like a snake, Mama."

"Oh, goodness, don't get too close to snakes, Coretta Emily. You must try to stay away from dangerous situations."

"Yes, ma'am."

"Lerryn, dear, how long have I been sleeping?"

"Off and on for about two days, Mama."

"My word . . . well, help me sit up, won't you?"

Lerryn scooted to her mother's side. "Are you sure you feel like it?"

"Certainly. Sometimes I just need some sleep."

Lerryn took hold of her mother's hand. "Mama, I think you should take it easy."

Retta watched as Lerryn gently raised Mrs. Barre.

"Oh dear, I am a little dizzy still. I'll wait to cook supper until my head clears."

"Mama, are you feeling better?" Retta asked.

"I believe I do need to take it easy." She patted Lerryn's hand. "I trust I didn't act like a pill again."

"Mama, you're always the lady," Lerryn assured her.

"And you're a beautiful, loyal daughter."

"How about me, Mama?" Retta pressed.

"Oh, Coretta, you make my heart sing just to look at you in that—that outfit. The Lord has blessed me so abundantly with fine children. I'm a fortunate woman."

"I can cook supper for us tonight," Lerryn offered.

"And I'll help her, Mama. Let us do it," Retta pleaded.

"Why don't you leave me a basin of water so I can wash up."

"Are you goin' to be all right by yourself if we go cook?"

"Oh, darlin', I trust so. I suppose you should cook a little of that dreadful salt pork. Did we have it for breakfast? Funny, I can't remember breakfast. I don't remember much of anything. When did the other wagons leave?"

"Yesterday morning, Mother," Lerryn reported.

"Papa went to the river to hunt us some game. We'll have fresh meat," Retta said.

"He did? Oh that dear, dear, sweet Eugene. Girls, if you ever find a man like your Papa, you should marry him instantly."

"But, Mama, I'm only twelve," Retta objected.

Mrs. Barre studied her youngest daughter. "Li'l sis, you've grown up on this trip. I do believe you left Ohio a little girl and will arrive in Oregon a young lady. Of course, you might have to wear a different dress in Oregon."

Lerryn stroked her mother's arm. "You have a beautiful smile, Mama."

"I love you, Mama," Retta blurted out.

"You girls and your brothers know how special you are to me. I love you more dearly than anything on earth. Now how about helping me to my feet?" Mrs. Barre requested.

"Mama, I don't think you should try to stand," Lerryn cautioned.

"I'd like to try. The quicker I regain my strength, the sooner we'll catch up with the others. Coretta Emily, come up here and help your sister pull me to my feet. Once I get the cobwebs out of my mind, I'll do just fine."

Retta glanced at Lerryn.

Lerryn shrugged.

Retta pulled herself up into the wagon.

"Now," Mrs. Barre instructed, "I'd like one of you under this arm."

Retta moved over, and Mrs. Barre put her arm around her daughter's shoulder. Lerryn moved under her mother's other arm.

"Okay, girls, lift me up."

With all their mother's weight draped on their shoulders, Retta and Lerryn tugged the woman to her feet.

"Now, see? That's not so bad. Now step back and let me stand on my own."

"Mama, this isn't a good idea," Lerryn insisted.

"What could possibly happen? Step back and let me stand on my own."

Retta watched Lerryn as they stepped backwards at the same time and let their mother go.

"You see . . ." Mrs. Barre began. Suddenly her knees buckled, and she collapsed on the bedrolls.

"Mama!" Lerryn hollered.

Mrs. Barre rolled over on her back and began to laugh.

"Are you hurt, Mama?" Retta called.

"No, baby, I'm fine," she snickered.

"Why are you laughing?"

"My demonstration of competence didn't turn out as expected. I believe the Lord healed my mind before He healed my legs. I'm quite embarrassed, but I'm glad that only my daughters had to witness such foolishness. I suppose you will need to help me up to the comforter."

Retta and Lerryn lifted their mother back up to the quilt and pillows.

"Eh, Mama," Lerryn said, "I think you're bleeding again."

Retta plucked up the shotgun.

"The same thing happened just about twelve and a half years ago. Lerryn, would you get me those rags?

Coretta, can you fetch me a basin of water? What are you doing with that gun?"

Retta pulled back the hammer of the shotgun. "Papa and the boys said to fire the gun if we need them."

Mrs. Barre brushed at the skirt of her dress. "I hardly think it's necessary."

"It would make me feel better, Mama, if Papa were here," Lerryn added.

"Well, all right, but I hope it doesn't scare poor Eugene to death. That sweet man has had to put up with a lot lately. You go on out in front of the wagon, li'l sis, and please be careful with that gun."

Retta scooted to the front of the wagon, but when she swung her leg up on the wagon seat, it tangled in a rope. She lost her balance and tumbled from the wagon, landing facedown in the dirt. The shotgun blasted when the butt stock hit the wagon tongue, her finger still on the trigger.

There was a distant scream and a curse. A bearded man staggered away from the rope corrals toward a waiting paneled wagon.

"That squaw done shot my backside, Elmo!" the man screamed. "Shoot her!"

"Serves you right, Davy. I told you not to take an Indian's cow. They is testy that way."

"Wait up for me, Elmo!" he screamed.

The wagon and the man disappeared over the rise.

Lerryn lunged out the front of the wagon.

"Is Retta all right?" Mrs. Barre called out.

"Yes, just a little mussed up," Lerryn replied.

"What was all that noise?" Mrs. Barre queried.

"I think it was one of those prairie pests, Mama," Retta hollered. "But don't worry—I chased him off."

She looked up to see two horses galloping from the river.

Five

$\mathcal{B}$y the time the sun sank below Laramie Peak far to the west, all four Barre children were huddled around the small chip fire next to the covered wagon. The breeze neither warmed nor cooled, but it did blow away most of the gnats and flies. Because of the bitter smoke, all four sat on the same side of the campfire.

Retta and Lerryn occupied the big green trunk, their feet barely touching the prairie dirt. When William looked back over his shoulder, the other three glanced back as well.

Mr. Barre climbed down out of the wagon and strolled over to them. His nearly white cotton shirt was unbuttoned, and his braces left shadowy vertical stripes on his chest. He carried a small oil lamp, shielding it with his other hand.

William stood, his own suspenders hanging off his shoulders and draping down his ducking trousers. "How's Mama?"

Mr. Barre set the lamp on a crate. "She's better. It's a blessin' from the Lord 'cause I surely wasn't expectin' it."

Andrew whittled on a short stick. The shavings tumbled into the fire. "Will we be able to leave in the morning?" he asked.

Mr. Barre began to pace through the drifting campfire

smoke. "Perhaps so, or perhaps the next day." A soft smile broke across his face. "She does seem to be on the mend."

"What about those prairie raiders that Retta chased off?" Andrew asked. "Will they cause us any more trouble?"

Mr. Barre held his finger to his lips and squatted down between his children and the small, smoldering fire. "Shhh, not too loud. I didn't have the heart to tell Mama about them yet."

"She still thinks I was just signaling you?" Retta whispered.

Mr. Barre reached over and patted her knee. "I reckon she does, darlin'."

"But what about the raiders, Papa?" Lerryn pressed.

"I surmise they'll either try to slip back here after dark," he said, rubbing his chin, "or push on to catch up with the wagon train. Thanks to li'l' sis, they think there are Indians at this wagon. If they were smart, they wouldn't come back. But I haven't heard any indication of much intelligence."

Andrew tossed the whittled stick into the fire and slipped his knife back into the sheath. "Do you really think they'll attack the wagon train?"

Mr. Barre stared into the fire. "Nope. If Retta heard right and they only have three men and a couple bullets, they can't roll right up and start shootin'. But they might try to weasel in and steal as much as they can. You know our folks will always give them a meal and an overnight stay."

William pulled his suspenders back up over his shoulders. "We need to warn them."

Mr. Barre fanned the coals of the fire with his hat. "We'll try to catch up as quick as we can, but it would be too risky to send one of you ahead. It's too dangerous out here alone. Besides, we need you all here so that we can keep Mama safe. If Retta dispatched the scoundrels, I reckon the colonel, Bobcat, and the others can do the same."

Retta reached over and held her sister's hand. "Lerryn helped me."

Lerryn flipped her blonde bangs out of her eyes. "You should have seen li'l sis clobber that man with her coup stick. She raised that rock hammer above her head and slammed it into his boot. I bet she broke a few toes."

"He shouldn't have touched me," she mumbled. "But I didn't mean to do it so hard. I just got mad."

"He was lucky I wasn't around with my rifle," William declared.

"Sounds like li'l sis took care of the shootin', too." Andrew grinned.

"Now that really was an accident. I didn't mean to shoot him in the rear end," Retta explained.

William pushed his spectacles high on his nose. "Just exactly where did you mean to shoot him, Coretta Emily?"

"I didn't even know he was out there."

Mr. Barre shoved his hat back on his head. "I don't surmise they'll attack us, but they might be angry enough to sneak back and try to steal a cow or an ox."

"Me and Andrew will sleep out by the cattle," William offered.

Mr. Barre shook his head. "Thanks, boys. I know you mean it, but I'll do the night guardin' if it's necessary," he insisted.

"Papa, you need to be close to Mama. When she takes a spell, she doesn't want anyone around but her Eugene," Lerryn cautioned.

"She's right, Papa," Retta said.

"But I can't . . ." Mr. Barre protested.

"We'll tie the horses to the wagon wheels," Andrew said.

"And me and li'l' sis will sleep under the wagon with the shotgun and coup stick!" Lerryn announced.

Mr. Barre stood up and towered above his seated children. "Absolutely not."

"Papa, you need to be in the wagon with Mama," Lerryn maintained. "If she takes a bad turn, you're the only one who can do anything about it."

"And if she's having a good night, you're still the one she wants with her," Retta said.

"That's absurd. I can't sleep in the wagon while my children are exposed to harm."

"We're all exposed to harm, Papa," William pointed out. "That canvas-covered wagon would not stop a bullet or an arrow. What makes you safe in there?"

"Well . . . well . . ."

"Come on, Papa," Andrew urged. "It'll make us feel like we're takin' care of you and Mama."

"But—but you are just children."

"You got to let us grow up sometime. William's twenty, and I'm seventeen," Andrew insisted.

"That's what you keep telling me," Mr. Barre said. "But li'l sis is only twelve, and there's no way—"

"Papa," Lerryn interrupted, "Coretta Emily has proved she can stand against Indians and prairie bandits. She has more experience than 90 percent of the men in the wagon train. I feel safer with her alongside me than I would having the likes of Mr. Landers or some of the rest of them."

Mr. Barre pulled off his hat and scratched his head. "What am I goin' to do with you four? You argue like your Mama. You aren't goin' to let up until I relent, are you?"

"Nope." Lerryn grinned.

"Well, just this one night."

"Good. You go to bed. I'll get things organized out here," William announced.

Mr. Barre stared at his eldest son. "I need to help."

"Go to bed, Papa," Retta insisted.

"Don't I need to put up camp?"

William shook his head. "Nope."

"I'll bring in the horses."

"Nope," Andrew put in.

"Well, I have to do something."

"Go up there and scrunch up next to Mama. That will make her the happiest woman on earth," Lerryn suggested.

Even in the dim light, Retta could see her father blush. "I reckon you're right," he muttered.

His shoulders were slumped, but there was a slight smile on his face as he picked up the oil lamp and hiked back to the wagon. Within moments all light inside the wagon was extinguished.

For the next hour the four Barre children loaded up the gear, brought in the horses, spread the canvas, and laid out quilt pallets for beds. Retta and Lerryn were lying on top of the quilts when the boys hiked back in from taking care of the cattle. William carried a ball of string. They huddled to make plans.

"Are you goin' to sleep fully dressed?" he asked his sisters.

"I was going to pull off my shoes and stockings," Lerryn replied. "Is that okay?"

"Sure. I figure on doing the same," Andrew said.

"I think I'll leave my moccasins on," Retta announced.

"Retta has her coup stick, and I'll have the shotgun," Lerryn added. "We should be protected."

Retta pointed at the string in her brother's hand. "What's Papa's survey twine for?"

William tugged his spectacles to the end of his nose and peered over the rims. "Figured I'd tie one end on my wrist and the other on one of you. We could use it for signals."

"Tie it on who?" Retta asked.

William, Andrew, and Lerryn answered in unison, "You."

"Oh, okay," Retta grinned. "Eh, what will the signals be?"

"One tug means nothing. I reckon we may do that just turnin' over," William explained. "Two tugs means to listen. Three tugs means to come here quietly. Four tugs means to make noise when you come."

Retta's eyes widened as she nodded. "Okay."

"And five tugs means wake up, sleepyhead, and fix breakfast," Andrew laughed.

Lerryn looked up at her blue-eyed, strong-shouldered oldest brother. "Are you worried?"

"No," William replied. He pushed his spectacles up on his nose and stared out into the black prairie night. "Actually just a little scared. It's one thing to brag about doin' somethin', but it's another to actually do it. I know we can do it with the Lord's help."

The boys went back out to the cattle. Their shadowy silhouettes soon disappeared in the darkness. Retta stretched out lengthwise under the wagon box on the cattle side. Lerryn lay alongside her on the river side. The ground felt hard. The night air had cooled some. The pillow felt gritty on Retta's face, and her neck felt grimy.

"Night, Lerryn," she whispered.

"Night, sis."

"No li'l sis?"

"Not anymore." Lerryn reached over and put her hand on Retta's arm.

Retta scrunched around so she could hold her sister's hand.

Sometime after midnight, with the quarter moon casting a glow on the prairie, Retta reached up to brush a fly off her face, but she couldn't touch her ear.

Her hand was held back.

And someone was tugging on it.

Or something.

"Two tugs." Retta raised up on her elbows and listened.

She thought she heard the wind rustle in the tall grass to the south of the wagon, but she couldn't feel any wind at all under it.

There were no voices.

No hoofbeats.

No coyotes.

No night birds.

No cows lowing.

No Papa snoring.

Nothing.

What does William hear? Or did he just turn over twice? Should I go out there? Should I wake up Lerryn? Or Papa?

Retta grabbed her coup stick and waited.

And waited.

Lying on her stomach, she propped herself up on her elbows and then dozed off.

A violent tug on the string yanked her hand out from under her head. She crashed to the pillow.

"One tug?" she muttered.

She yanked two times on the cord. The line was slack, like a fishing line when the lead breaks off on a submerged stump. She tugged again and wound up with a handful of twine.

Now what am I supposed to do? Lord, William didn't tell me what to do when the line broke. I reckon I should go out there, but am I supposed to sneak up? If I sneak up when they don't expect me, they might shoot at me. But if I make noise when I'm not supposed to . . . Lord, I wish Papa was awake. He'd know what to do. He'd barge right out there. That's what I'll do. I'll do what Papa would do.

She reached over to wake up her sister.

Of course, he wouldn't wake up Lerryn.

Lord, this is Retta. I'm really sleepy and not too sure what to do. So . . . You might want to send an extra angel to help out here, you know, just in case I do it wrong.

When she picked up her coup stick, she felt her fingers run across the beaded headband. She slipped it over her hair. The feather tickled her ear.

The quarter moon stalled above her in the black, star-lit sky. Retta could see outlines of the cattle and silhouettes of horses as she quietly approached.

There aren't supposed to be any horses out here. What's going on?

"Retta! Watch—" William's mumble was suddenly cut off.

Goosebumps sprang up on her neck and arms. "William? Andrew? What is it? Where are you? I can't see."

A light flickered behind her. She whipped around. A barefoot Lerryn plodded across the prairie, shotgun over her arm, a fat white candle in her hand. "What is it, Retta?" As Lerryn approached, her eyes widened, and she gasped, "Oh, no."

Retta spun back around. In the candlelight she spied Andrew and William held at knife point by half a dozen Indians with painted faces. William's leather suspenders were off his shoulders and hanging from his ducking trousers. His spectacles were missing. Both boys were barefoot.

Retta raised her coup stick as if to strike.

The one holding his hand over William's mouth and a knife to his throat dropped his hands and stepped closer.

"Careful, Retta," William croaked.

The Indian growled, "Red Bear?"

Retta nodded her head and squatted down in the middle of the group of Indians.

Lerryn held the candle over her shoulder. "What're you doing, Coretta?"

"Just hold the light," Retta ordered. *Lord, this is me, Retta, and I'm sort of in over my head again. I think I need that extra angel now.*

The main Indian squatted down beside her.

She pointed to her chest and then at the coup stick. "Red Bear." Her voice squeaked. She cleared her throat and repeated it louder. "I'm Red Bear!" It came out as a shout, and the Indian flinched back.

Then he nodded. "Red Bear."

Retta pointed to William, Andrew, the cattle and oxen, and then pointed to her chest.

"Belong to Red Bear?" the Indian mumbled.

She nodded her head. "Yes."

"And me—I belong to Red Bear," Lerryn called out from behind her.

Retta pointed to her sister and then back to herself. "Belong to Red Bear."

The Indian nodded. A smile crept across his face. He pointed back toward the covered wagon a hundred feet away.

Retta nodded. "Belong to Red Bear!"

The Indian said several words to his companions, ending with the words, "Red Bear."

They released Andrew and handed the boys back their rifles. Then the Indian waved to one of the others and said something. The man retrieved something from a belt pouch and handed it to the squatting Indian.

Retta studied the item in the man's hands. "Oh no," she whispered over her shoulder.

"What's the matter? What is it? I can't see." Lerryn stepped closer.

"It's a beautiful bone choker. He's going to give it to me."

The Indian leaned forward and held the three-strand necklace to her neck. Then he reached around and tied it behind her neck.

There was a mumbling of approval among the Indians.

"But I have to give him something," Retta groaned. "I—I don't have anything."

William unbuttoned his leather suspenders and handed them to Retta.

"I can't give him your braces," she said.

"Do it. I don't want to give them a gun," William replied.

"But he doesn't have buttons on his buckskins," Lerryn pointed out.

"He'll figure out something," Andrew told her.

Retta folded the braces and presented them to the Indian. Then she pointed to her chest. "Belong to you . . . from Red Bear."

He reached over and held her left arm just below the shoulder. She put her right hand on his muscled bare left arm just below his shoulder.

He nodded.

She nodded.

The Indian stood and in the candlelight laid the braces over his bare shoulders with the crossed piece over his chest.

"No," Retta said. She motioned for him to bend down just a little. She turned the braces so they crossed his bare back and hung straight down in front. Then she pointed to where they should be fastened on his trousers. "You must fix buttons!"

He stood tall, threw his shoulders back, and strutted in front of the other Indian men. They laughed and began speaking all at once. Then as if on cue, they mounted their horses. The main Indian pointed to the cows and then in the direction of the covered wagon. "Belong to Red Bear."

"Yes," she called out. "Good-bye!"

"Good," the man called out in the dark. "Good."

For a minute she could hear their hoofbeats and then silence again. The four stood in the flickering light of Lerryn's candle.

"I reckon they're Cheyenne," Retta murmured. "But they looked different from Dance-with-the-Sun."

William cleared his throat. "Was this a bad dream, or did it really happen?"

Andrew stepped up alongside of him. "I've never been so scared in my life."

"I was so scared I . . ." Lerryn bit her lip and grimaced. "I need to go back and change clothes."

William put his arm on Retta's shoulder. "You keep bailin' us out, sis."

"Dance-with-the-Sun told me to show other Indians this coup stick. I didn't really know what I was doing."

"Are you kidding me?" William said. "You knew exactly what to do and say."

"Ah, the legends of Coretta Emily Barre." Andrew stepped up to her other side. "Someday there will be a book written about her."

Retta felt her face flush. "That's a laugh."

"No, it's true," Lerryn said. "I think I'll write it."

"I keep thinking I'm testing the Lord," Retta replied. "I hope He doesn't get tired of rescuing me."

"Looks like He's not tired yet," William remarked as he tugged up his trousers.

Six

The eastern sky had turned light gray when Retta woke up. Her back hurt. Her right hand was numb from the pinch of the rawhide strap of the coup stick. The eagle feather stuck under the collar of her dress. Her toes throbbed from the cold. The acrid smell of a chip fire filled the air. She sat up and bumped her head on the wagon box. Rubbing her head, Retta crawled out from under the wagon and struggled to her feet.

"Mornin', darlin'," her father greeted her.

"Hi, Papa! I could have started the fire."

"I figured you could sleep in." He licked his fingers and brushed down her wild hair. "How're you feelin'?"

"Wonderful . . . now." Retta grinned.

Mr. Barre glanced around the prairie. "Looks like you all had a peaceful night. The boys just took the livestock to the river to water them. You four must be gettin' used to sleepin' on the ground."

Retta stretched her arms and rubbed her back. "Sometimes I wake up in the middle of the night, but I can usually get back to sleep."

"Did you wake up last night?"

"Eh, just once, Papa."

"I slept better than I have in weeks."

She rubbed her hands in the pan of water and splashed some on her face. "Is Mama awake yet?"

Mr. Barre glanced back at the wagon. "I don't think so, but you can go check."

Retta climbed up on the covered wagon seat and then into the back.

"Mama?" she whispered.

Her mother opened her eyes and held out her arms. "Mornin', Coretta! How's my Indian princess? Oh, look at you! What a beautiful necklace. Have I seen that before?"

Retta crawled over some crates to hug her mother, who felt warm and a little sweaty. There was a hint of menthol in the air. "This is the first day I've worn it," she replied.

"I suppose one of your Indian friends gave it to you."

Retta stroked her mother's thin cheek. "Yes."

Mrs. Barre took her daughter's hand. "I must have slept through that part."

"I reckon you did."

Mrs. Barre pulled Retta's fingers to her lips and kissed them. "I can't believe I slept through two whole days."

Retta returned the kiss to her mother's fingers. "You needed the rest, Mama."

"Will you hand me my brown dress? It's the only one I own that still fits. I'm getting very tired of living in a cotton gown."

Retta retrieved the dress for her mother. "Are we going to try to catch up with the wagon train today?"

"We'll get back on the trail, but we won't catch them in one day. That is, we'll start moving if you can convince your father to go," Mrs. Barre replied.

"Me?"

"He insists that I should rest one more day, but I know that we fall farther behind each hour that we wait. I feel confident that I can get along fine, but he won't listen to me. So you and big sis will have to talk him into it. You two can talk him into anything." She motioned Retta closer.

"Mama, everyone knows you have him wrapped around your little finger."

Mrs. Barre pulled her close, licked her fingers, and tried to smooth down Retta's errant bangs. "Coretta Emily, let me tell you something. No man was ever wrapped around a woman's finger unless he wanted to be."

Retta mashed her bangs down with her hand and held them against her forehead. "I'll go get breakfast started."

Mrs. Barre pulled herself to a sitting position. "Wake up your sister to help."

"I'm awake," Lerryn called out from under the wagon.

Mrs. Barre spoke loudly enough for both girls to hear. "I understand you two girls were responsible for making Papa sleep in the wagon last night."

"I guess so," Lerryn replied.

"Well, someday when you're both happily married and have your own children," a coy smile rolled across Mrs. Barre's thin lips as she finished, "you'll know what a precious gift that was."

"That makes me happy, Mama," Retta replied.

"And it makes me happy that the Lord took such good care of my children last night. He is indeed good, isn't He?"

William rode scout almost a mile in front of the wagon.

Andrew drove the extra cattle between the wagon and the river.

Mr. Barre walked beside the oxen with the bullwhip.

They propped Mrs. Barre up on quilts in the wagon seat.

Lerryn and Retta hiked upwind from the dust of the slow-moving procession. There were very few buffalo chips to gather, but the girls toted burlap chip bags just in case.

With the sun straight above them, the worn soil of the trail reflected the summer heat.

Lerryn wore pale green calico and a matching bonnet.

Retta wore her buckskins, eagle-feather headband, bone necklace, and moccasins.

"Lerryn, did you ever kiss a boy and not mean it?" Retta blurted out.

Lerryn's dancing blue eyes sparkled. "Not mean what?"

Retta puffed out her cheeks. The bone choker necklace felt tight on her throat. "Joslyn said she kissed this boy in Missouri a few times, but she had never kissed a boy and meant it. Did you ever kiss a boy and not mean it?"

Lerryn cupped her hand at Retta's ear and whispered, "You want to know the truth? Brian is the only boy I ever kissed."

"What about Chet Martin?"

"No."

"Ellis LeBayne?"

"No."

"Abner Crossier?"

"No."

"Surely you kissed Jimmy Trooper?"

"That was the sixth grade."

"But you said he was your boyfriend."

"That was the summer Papa took us all to Texas."

"Was he too old?"

"No. He was too bashful."

"He could play the fiddle and sing."

"Yes, he could."

The two sisters paused and stared at a flat brown object on the dirt.

"It's your turn," Lerryn announced.

"I picked up the last one," Retta objected. "And the one before that and the one before that."

"You're more experienced than me."

Retta reached down and scooped up the dried buffalo dropping.

"Here," Lerryn offered, "you can put it in my sack. That way you don't have to carry them all."

"That way Papa will think you actually touched one."

Lerryn giggled, "You're a pal!"

"I'm a sucker," Retta sighed as she shoved the buffalo chip into her sister's burlap sack.

They hiked in silence for several minutes. The only sounds were the crack of Mr. Barre's whip and the squeak of the wagon wheels.

Lerryn spoke first. "Retta, have you ever kissed a boy and not meant it?"

Retta felt her face flush. She puffed out her cheeks and held her breath. Finally she announced, "You know I've never kissed a boy."

Lerryn poked her with her elbow. "Not even Ben Weaver?"

Retta sucked in her breath. "Especially Ben Weaver. I would never kiss him."

"Why not?"

"He might think that I like him," Retta declared.

"You *do* like him, don't you?" Lerryn challenged.

"Yes, but I wouldn't want him to think . . . you know."

"No, what?" Lerryn grinned.

"You know."

"Impure thoughts?"

Retta lowered her chin to her chest. "Yeah."

"That's very considerate of you."

"Okay, so no boys ever wanted to kiss me. But if they ever do, I'll just say, 'not unless you really mean it.'"

Lerryn broke out laughing. She put her arm around Retta's shoulder. "You're a fun sister. Where have you been all my life?"

"Across the table kicking your shins, spilling milk on your new dress," Retta reminded her.

Lerryn let her hand slip down into Retta's. "You know what I think?"

"What?"

"I think gettin' left back on our own for a few days is the nicest thing the Lord could have done for us."

"Mama looks better, doesn't she?"

"Yes, she does."

"Lerryn, why do you think Mama has her spells?"

"I don't know."

Retta stared up at a white cloud cruising the pale blue sky. "Other women go through the same thing and never have spells like that."

"I know. It makes me wonder what you and I will be like when it's our turn."

Retta giggled. "I don't really think about that very much. I'm not sure I'll ever have a turn."

"Well, that's good." Lerryn smiled. "Because I was afraid for a while you were going to run off and marry an Indian chief."

Retta took Lerryn's arm and skipped along. "That warrior last night was really strong. Did you see his muscles?"

"Yes, and I saw your eyes when you held on to his arm."

"I didn't hold on to his arm. That was just a greeting. Sort of like shaking hands."

"And when he tied on the necklace?"

Retta felt her face blush. "Now I'm starting to look like a real Red Bear."

"Hmmmm," Lerryn said.

"What did that mean?" Retta queried.

"It means I'm laughing at you, sweet sister."

Andrew rode over to them. "You two seem to be havin' fun."

"I'm telling li'l sis all about boys," Lerryn said.

"Well, Retta, what're you learnin' from the queen of the wagon train?" her brother probed.

"How to kiss," Retta declared.

"What?" he gasped.

Retta held her suntanned nose in the air. "I'm not going to wait around for you or William to tell me."

"You're only twelve," he scoffed.

"And how old were you when you first kissed a girl and meant it?" Lerryn probed.

"That's not the point," he said scowling.

"How old?"

"William was almost seventeen."

"I didn't ask about William."

Andrew sat back in the saddle. "Look, I didn't come over here to discuss kissing."

Lerryn slipped her arm into Retta's. "Why did you come over here?"

"Papa said one of you could ride Prince and push the cattle along. He wants me to ride up and get a report from William."

Retta studied the western horizon. "I don't see big brother."

"That's why Papa wants me to check on him."

"We'll both ride Prince," Lerryn declared.

Retta stopped and stared at her sister's blue eyes. "We will?"

"Yes! Bareback." Lerryn tugged her toward the wagon. "It'll be fun."

Retta trailed along after her sister. "We haven't ridden together since I was five."

"Yes, and why did we quit?" Lerryn asked.

"I think it had something to do with me throwing up all over you and Brownie, and he bucked us off, and you said you'd never ride with me again."

"That was a long time ago," Lerryn declared. "However, you're riding in front."

Prince paid little attention to the two girls on his back as he herded the two spare oxen, two milk cows, a spindly legged calf, and two steers.

"I like it up here," Retta announced. "I can see a lot farther across the prairie grass."

Lerryn wrapped her arms around Retta's waist. "Can you see William and Andrew?"

"No," Retta declared. "Papa said if we see anyone ride up, we have to turn and ride sidesaddle."

"These past couple of days have been like a vacation."

"Last night was a nightmare. Don't you think we should tell Papa?"

Prince stumbled, and Lerryn clutched Retta tighter. "Only if he asks."

"What're we goin' to do tonight? Will we ask Papa to go inside?"

"I don't know. The boys said they would keep the livestock close to the wagon, and so it'll be different."

"There's William," Retta shouted.

"Where's Andrew?"

"I guess he stayed out in front. William's probably riding back because he has something to tell Papa."

They watched as William pulled up to the oxen team and talked to his father. Then he turned and rode over toward them. "Hey, look at the drover girls," he called out as he approached. "Retta, from a distance you surely do look Indian! Lookin' at you two purdy gals made me realize that every boy on the prairie, Indian or white, is jealous of me and Andrew."

"Now, Retta," Lerryn giggled, "you just watch out for that kind of talk from a young man. That means he's trying to get you to do something."

"What do you want me to do?" Retta queried.

"Whoa, you're gettin' bum advice, li'l sis. I merely came over here to tell you and Papa that if we cross the river to the north, we can save ten miles off the trip and catch up with the wagon train a day earlier."

"I thought Mr. Bouchet said never to go on the north side of the river because that makes the Indians angry," Lerryn maintained.

"That's true," William chuckled, "but we have Red Bear with us, and so it'll be all right. Besides, the Mormons travel on the north side of the North Platte."

"I'm serious, William," Lerryn challenged.

"So am I. Papa said that if the river looks fordable, we would do that."

"When could we catch up?" Retta asked.

"Sometime tomorrow evening."

Lerryn clapped her hands. "That would be wonderful."

"Now I need you girls to do something for me."

"Aha, what did I tell you?" Lerryn laughed.

"What do you want us to do?" Retta asked.

"I'm goin' to stay with the cattle. I want you to ride over that next rise and then drop down to your right. You'll see two dead cottonwoods near the river. Ride up there."

"Then what?" Retta asked.

"Andrew's waiting for you."

"Why?"

"To show you something."

"What?" Lerryn probed.

"Go on, he'll show you."

"It better not be a snake or something like that," Lerryn warned.

"Now, big sis, go on."

"If it's a snake, I'm goin' to put it in your bedroll," Lerryn declared.

William slapped Prince's flanks. The big brown horse broke into a trot and kept that pace all the way to the top of the rise. When they crested, they could see the winding course of the river and the two dead cottonwoods. As they approached, they saw a couple of horses.

"There's Andrew," Retta called out. "But someone must be with him."

Lerryn stared over Retta's shoulder. "I can't see anyone."

"That's a beautiful pinto!" Retta cried. "Do you think Andrew and William found a horse out here on the prairie? It's chestnut and white."

"No one finds a tame horse on the prairie." Lerryn leaned her chin on Retta's shoulder blade. "Not with prairie pirates and Indians all over."

"Andrew," Retta called as they rode up, "where did you find that beautiful horse?"

Andrew pulled off his hat and grinned. "William found him right here."

"Really?" Retta's voice cracked. "Was he hard to catch? Is he wild?"

"Easy to catch." He pointed to the horse's fetlock. "He was picketed."

Retta slipped off Prince and felt her moccasins mash into the soft prairie soil. "Someone just up and left him staked to the prairie? Who would do that? He's a beautiful horse."

"That's why we sent for you. There's some Indian writin' on the dirt. We figured you could cipher it." Andrew winked at Lerryn.

"What does it say?" Retta questioned.

"There are just some pictures. Come here and read it for us."

Retta walked by the pinto and stroked his neck and then scratched behind his ears. "Did you ever see such a beautiful chestnut-and-white horse?"

"Nope, I don't reckon I did." Andrew pointed to the ground. "There it is."

Retta walked around and squatted by the markings.

"It's Two Bears's drawing. Look, there're his two little bears. It must be his horse."

"No, I don't think so." Andrew pointed to a different drawing in the dirt. "Look at this."

"That's a paint horse . . . and that's a buffalo. I've seen him draw them before."

"I think it means horse equals buffalo."

"You mean, we have to eat this horse like a buffalo?" Retta gasped.

"I don't think so." Andrew took her hand and pointed to a different symbol. "What do you think this is?"

"A red bear? That's me!"

Andrew took her arm, and they both stood up. "Li'l sis, Two Bears traded you this horse for your buffalo."

"No, that's not what it means," Retta insisted.

"Yes, it is."

"How do you know?"

"Because Two Bears told me so. He's right up there at the river, movin' his family across."

"You mean, it's my horse?"

"Yep."

"It's *really* my horse?"

"Yep."

"My very own? I own him?"

"He belongs to you. What do you think?"

"I think I'm goin' to cry!" She turned around to look at Lerryn, who sat grinning on Prince. "He's *my* horse," she sobbed.

"I know, Coretta Emily." Lerryn tucked her blonde hair back under her bonnet. "Now you'll have to think of a name for him."

Retta threw her arms around the pinto's neck and hugged him. "I already have a name for him. I've had a name picked out since I was five."

"What's that?" Lerryn asked. "What're you goin' to call him?"

Retta puffed out her cheeks and then roared, "His name is Muggins."

Seven

Retta thought it was probably the best feeling in the world.

The easterly wind blew her hair straight back.

Hooves thundered across the prairie.

She bounced in unison with the nine hundred pounds of horseflesh beneath her.

The sun was hot.

The air dry.

The sky blue.

Life was wonderful.

From the back of Muggins.

She tugged on the rope reins as she pulled up to the river. A group of Indians rode and waded across the shallow river.

"Two Bears," she hollered.

The brown-skinned, lean-muscled man at the river's edge turned and smiled. "Ah, Red Bear, you have come home." He held an arm up to her.

She slid down the off-side of the pinto and jogged over to him. "Now don't you start pretending I'm your daughter." Retta threw her arms around the man. "Two Bears, thank you for my horse."

He hugged her back and grinned. "Is this not the way you hug your father?"

"Yes, it is. But you'll just have to get used to the idea that I'm not going to live with you," she blurted out in laughter.

Two Bears rubbed his chin as if contemplating the future of the buffalo on the great plains. "I shall have to live in sadness." He grinned.

She ran back over to the horse that stood quietly on the prairie, his rope reins lying on the ground. "Isn't Muggins the most beautiful horse in the world?" she shouted.

Two Bears walked over to her. "His name is Muggins?"

Retta danced around him. "Oh, yes!"

"That is strange." Two Bears grabbed the startled horse's nose and stared straight into the big eyes. "He never told me his name was Muggins."

She threw her arms around the poll of the horse. "When I was a little girl, I dreamed that I would one day own a pinto, and his name would be Muggins."

"And now your dream has come true."

She watched as Two Bears thrust his fingers into his mouth and whistled loudly. Across the river three horses emerged from the water and then stopped dead in their tracks.

She put her arm into his. "You're an angel."

Two Bears raised his black eyebrows. "Does your God allow Shoshone to be angels?"

"Oh, yes." Retta clapped her hands. "He's quite tolerant, you know."

Still surveying the crossing, he nodded. "Yes, I have heard that."

Retta crawled back up on the back of the pinto. "Why don't you and your family travel with us?"

"Where are you going?"

She leaned back, her hand on Muggins's rump. "To catch up with the wagon train. Where're you going?"

Two Bears once again studied the river. "To almost catch up with the wagon train."

By early afternoon the mixed procession plodded west across the trackless prairie on the north side of the river. William, Two Bears, and Retta led the way. Then came the Barre wagon. Mr. Barre kept the oxen moving. Lerryn rode on the wagon seat with her quilting in her hands. Mrs. Barre lay on blankets inside the covered wagon. Then came a line of three travois led by Lucy Two Bears carrying her baby on her back, then the remuda of Indian horses, and finally Andrew and the Barre cattle.

Shy Bear walked alongside the covered wagon, wearing her pansy-plum gingham dress and bonnet. One of her smaller brothers rode the lead ox and kept up a running unintelligible conversation with Mr. Barre.

About an hour before sundown, they pulled over to the treeless river near thick brush and made camp. Two Bears's wife and children set up their two conical tents across from the covered wagon. A community fire was built between the two camps. When the joint meal had been cooked, Lerryn and Retta helped Mrs. Barre climb down out of the wagon.

"Are you sure it's safe to camp with . . . your friends, Coretta?" she whispered.

"I imagine that's exactly what Two Bears's wife is asking him right now," Retta replied.

"I suppose we're all fearful of what is different," Mrs. Barre murmured.

"They aren't all that different. They like fresh meat, sunny days, and fast horses," Retta remarked.

"Yes, well, that being the case, I can see how compatible we are." Mrs. Barre released a grin, and wrinkles melted from around her eyes. "Darlin', if only I could see the world through your eyes every day. You have such a delightful gift of happiness."

When everyone had huddled around the fire and the

cooking pots, Two Bears held up his hands. "I will speak for my family since most cannot speak your language. We thank you for allowing us to travel with Red Bear and her family. She makes us smile, and we are grateful for that. And now Red Bear will pray for us." He bowed his head, and instantly the whole Shoshone family lowered their heads.

"Me?" Retta gulped.

"Go ahead, darlin'," Mr. Barre prodded.

Retta bowed her head. "Eh, Lord . . . this is Coretta Emily . . . again . . . and this is my family and my good friends . . . Well, they're all sort of my family. . . . Please bless this food, even though I don't know what's in the brown bowl, but I'll probably try to eat it anyway. And keep Mama feeling good, and may we catch up with the wagon train tomorrow, and I sort of hope Ansley kept her word about Ben. In Jesus' name, amen."

Lerryn sidled up next to her as they scooped food on their plates.

"Did that sound dumb?" Retta asked. "I didn't know what to say, and so I just said what was on my mind."

Lerryn leaned her shoulder against Retta's. "So you're worried about Ben?"

"When they pulled out, I thought I might never see any of them again. But if we do catch up tomorrow, well," Retta said, rolling her eyes, "I reckon I'd like to visit with him."

Lerryn pointed to the brown pot. "What is this stuff?" she whispered.

"I don't know," Retta whispered back. "Two Bears said it would be better if I didn't know." Retta scooped some of the lumpy white mash onto her plate. She stabbed one of the lumps with her fork and popped it into her mouth.

"What does it taste like?" Lerryn asked.

"Mmmmmphth." Retta swallowed hard. "Oh, sort of halfway between lima beans . . . and chicken."

People sat on crates, quilts, and buffalo robes as they ate. There was a steady drone of conversation and laughter, though the families were unable to communicate much with each other. Mrs. Two Bears nursed her baby at the entrance to one of the lodges.

It didn't cool off when the sun went down, but the wind picked up a little. Mrs. Barre went back inside the covered wagon. After dark the fire was built up. Two Bears told a long story about Jim Bridger, speaking a line in English and then in Shoshone. When he finished, everyone laughed.

Then Shy Bear stood. With her chin on her chest, she stared at the coals in the fire and began to sing a chant. The other family members joined in.

When she finished, the Barre family all clapped. Retta stood and began to sing "Amazing Grace." First Lerryn and then William and Andrew came beside her and sang. As soon as they concluded, Two Bears's family whistled and shouted.

Then Shy Bear began another Shoshone chant.

This was followed by another hymn from the Barre family, and the song exchange continued for almost an hour. When Two Bears began his third Jim Bridger story, Shy Bear tugged on Retta's sleeve. Retta trailed the Indian girl to the edge of the camp where the horses were picketed. Shy Bear took Retta straight to the pinto.

"Isn't he beautiful?" Retta whispered. In the background she could hear Two Bears telling his story. The Indian borrowed William's rifle for the part about Bridger shooting an elk near an obsidian mountain.

Shy Bear pointed to the horse's back.

"You want to ride him with me?" Retta pointed to Shy Bear, then to herself, and then to the horse.

The Indian girl nodded.

"Give me a boost." Retta grabbed the horse's mane and jumped up on his back as Shy Bear shoved her up.

Retta reached down her hand. "Come on!"

Shy Bear leaped and caught Retta's arm with both hands. The weight of the Indian girl's body pulled Retta off the horse, and she landed on top of Shy Bear. Both girls began to laugh.

Until a strong arm grabbed Retta's shoulder. A pistol was shoved in her side.

"Unhand that white girl," the deep voice growled.

Shy Bear's eyes grew wide as she lay on her back on the ground. Retta puffed out her cheeks and twisted her head. In the shadows she spied an army lieutenant with a light brown goatee.

Retta stood up and brushed down her buckskin dress. "We're just playing."

The officer spoke softly. "You speak English?"

Retta wiggled her nose. "My name is Retta Emily Barre from Barresville, Ohio, and we're on our way to Oregon City, Oregon. Who are you?"

He pulled off his hat and scratched his blond head. "You're not Indian?"

"No, Shy Bear's the Indian." She reached down and helped the girl to her feet.

Shy Bear looked up at the uniformed man and then hid behind Retta.

The man scratched his neck and lowered the gun. "What's going on here?"

"I told you, we're on our way to Oregon. Shy Bear and her family are only going to Fort Bridger."

"You're traveling together?"

"Yes, but our wagon train is up ahead. We had to lag back because Mama was sick. . . . Well, she's still sick but feeling much better, thank you. So we crossed the river to catch up, and Two Bears—they're Shoshone, you know—well, he and his family are friends of mine. They gave me this dress. Actually Shy Bear and I traded dresses. I must admit I got the best of the deal. So we're traveling together, and we camped here for the night, and we were all singing, except for mother. She's in the wagon because she needs the rest. Then Two Bears decided to tell a long story. He likes to tell long stories, but Shy Bear and me came over to see Muggins. That's my horse. My very own horse. Isn't he the most beautiful horse in the world? And we came over to ride him, and I climbed up and tried to help Shy Bear, but I fell off on top of her, and we were having fun and laughing until you stopped us."

Retta paused and puffed out her cheeks. "Who are you, and why are you here?" she asked.

Another soldier stepped up beside the lieutenant. "My word, you are an American all right. Are you telling me that you're traveling with these savages?" the private muttered.

"No, I said we're traveling with friends." She turned to the officer. "You didn't answer my question."

"I'm Lieutenant Rogers from Fort Laramie. My company is looking for a renegade Arapaho who has been causing trouble."

Retta put her arm around the cowering Shy Bear. "You're looking for Tall Owl?"

The officer looked startled. "You've seen him?"

"Oh my, yes. But I'm afraid Dance-with-the-Sun and some other Cheyenne have him now," Retta responded.

"Dance-with-the-Sun is a hundred miles north of here," the lieutenant reported.

"I don't think so," Retta countered.

"Li'l sis," Mr. Barre hollered, "are you talkin' to your horse again?"

She walked over to where she could see her father. "No,

Papa, I'm talkin' to some army men. Can they come in by the fire and have some coffee?"

Mr. Barre stood to his feet. "How many of them are there?"

Retta turned back to the lieutenant. "How many men do you have?"

The lieutenant jammed on his hat. "Just thirty."

"They got thirty, Papa," she yelled toward the campfire.

"In that case," Mr. Barre said, looking over at Two Bears, "we'll have to make more coffee."

Retta awoke in an encampment that bustled with activity.

Soldiers.

Indians.

Her father and brothers.

"Mornin', darlin'," Mr. Barre called out. "How did you sleep?"

"I think it was the best night's rest since we left Missouri." Retta crawled off the quilts.

"Surprisin' how peaceful it feels when surrounded by the U.S. Army. Big sis is over there, of course." He pointed to a huddle of uniformed soldiers.

Retta held out the front of her buckskin dress and scraped off some dried white gravy with her thumbnail. "Lerryn's up already?"

Mr. Barre moseyed over to Retta. "Eh, she was up before daylight. She put on that satin dress and curled her hair."

"Her satin dress? Mama said she couldn't wear that dress until we get to Oregon." Retta licked at something sticky and sweet stuck between her fingers.

"Don't know anything about that," Mr. Barre declared. "But tell her to come help you cook breakfast. The lieutenant is eatin' with us, and I don't want Mama to have to cook."

Retta tugged on her moccasins, smoothed down her buckskin dress, and slipped on her headband. She washed her hands in the basin and patted down her thick, wild hair with her wet hands. She strolled through the busy encampment, tying on her bone necklace as she approached the circle of men. They parted when she arrived.

"Oh, and this is my little sister," Lerryn announced.

"Your sister is an Indian, Miss Lerryn?" one young soldier called out.

"Oh, no." Lerryn grinned. "That's just a costume. She doesn't wear it all the time."

"Sort of like Lerryn's satin dress," Retta sniped. "It's just a costume. She doesn't wear it all the time."

"Don't you have something to do?" Lerryn huffed.

"Yes, and so do you," Retta said. "We have to cook breakfast."

"Oh, can't you do that?" Lerryn paused. Then a smile replaced her frown. She stepped over and slipped her arm into her startled sister's. "Now, boys," Lerryn drawled, "my sis and I have some chores to take care of. You'll just have to do something besides flirt with us!"

Retta could feel herself blush.

A young blond man with a corporal's stripe tipped his hat. "You have an unforgettable smile, Miss Lerryn."

"Oh, posh, Tyler, you'll forget me as soon as you get to St. Louis. But don't any of you forget my sis's name." She stepped back and bowed. "This is my sister, Retta Barre, and someday you're going to read a book about her."

The girls giggled all the way back to the wagon.

"Why did you tell them that?" Retta asked.

"It just dawned on me when we were starting to snipe at each other that I don't have my heart in it anymore. I like it better when we get along."

"Mama told me last night that she thinks the Lord's

changing our hearts," Retta said. "Do you think that's what's happening?"

Lerryn's satin dress swished as they strolled across the camp. "Maybe that's it. All I know is that in the midst of visiting with the soldiers, I realized that I probably won't see any of them again, and I hope to see you most every day of the rest of my life. Boys come and go, but sisters . . ." Lerryn paused and wrinkled her narrow nose.

Retta raised her dark brown eyebrows. "You're stuck with forever?"

"Yes," Lerryn giggled. They paused by the fire. "What do you need me to do first?"

Retta fingered the smooth green material on her sister's sleeve. "Change this beautiful dress before you get it splattered with grease."

Eight

When they finally broke camp, the soldiers crossed the river and turned west. Two Bears and the Barre covered wagon headed due west on the north side of the river. The wind picked up by 9:00 A.M., and by 10:00 the dust began to roll off the dry soil.

Retta rode Muggins bareback into the wind alongside William and Two Bears. They didn't stop at noon even though the wind grew stronger.

"Three days ago we were stuck in the mud, and now look at this dust!" Retta shouted.

"Yes, but there are no bugs," Two Bears hollered back.

"How close to the other side of the river will the wagon train be?" she called out.

"Don't reckon the trail is along the river," William answered. "Most times of the year it would be too boggy for an entire wagon train."

"We can cross the river in about three miles," Two Bears reported.

"What will we do after that?" Retta asked.

"We could cut across the trail and see if the wagon train is up ahead or behind," William proposed.

"Do you really think we could have caught up with them by now?" Retta hollered into the wind.

William rode closer and leaned toward his sister. "This

is a very good shortcut, but we have to cross the river twice. Don't reckon it's too practical when the water is high or if a hundred wagons have to go across. I do think we can catch up."

"I can't wait to show off Muggins!" Retta flopped down along the horse's neck and patted his nose.

William wiped dust off his spectacles with his bandanna. "Oh, just who're you thinkin' of impressing?"

"Oh, you know—Christen, Joslyn, Gilson . . ."

"How about Miss Ansley?" he asked.

Retta curled her lower lip down. She glanced over at the Shoshone. "Two Bears, do you think Muggins can outrun Ansley's black horse?"

"Only for a short distance. He is very fast between the lodge and the river, but I don't think he will want to run long distances."

A scream from the wagon halted the caravan. Retta raced back. She felt Muggins's back slap across her sore behind. Lerryn knelt on the wagon seat peering inside. Retta dropped the reins and hit the ground running. "Is it Mama?"

Lerryn turned around. "Yes, Papa is with her."

Retta tried to see inside, but the wind-blown dust made her squint her eyes almost closed. "Did she have another spell?"

Lerryn turned around and sat down on the seat. "I just think it's her time."

"Really?"

"Yes."

"But we aren't at Fort Laramie. We were supposed to be at Fort Laramie." Retta puffed out her cheeks. "What does Papa want us to do?"

Lerryn climbed down next to her. "Just wait, I guess."

"It's a horribly windy day," Retta objected. "I wish we would press on until we find a windbreak."

Lerryn slipped her arm around Retta's waist as William rode up. "I suppose some things can't wait," she replied.

By the time Mr. Barre emerged, Andrew and William both stood beside their sisters.

"Lerryn, get up there with your mother," Mr. Barre commanded.

She climbed into the wagon.

Mr. Barre stepped toward his boys. "Unhook the oxen and drive them to the river to drink. We aren't goin' anywhere."

They began to pull the yokes off the livestock.

Two Bears parked his family at the river about a hundred yards away and waited.

Then Mr. Barre called to Retta, "Darlin', I'd like you to build a fire. Boilin' hot water will make a nice steam rag, but I don't know if you can get one going in this wind."

"I can do it, Papa," Retta shot back.

"Give it your best try, darlin'."

A fire proved more difficult than she had imagined. Even though Retta carved some shavings for a fire starter and used the big green trunk as a windbreak, every attempt failed.

A barefoot Shy Bear meandered over and viewed Retta's frantic efforts. Still wearing her pansy-plum dress, Shy Bear dropped to her knees and grabbed a stick. She began digging a very narrow trench with it.

"What're you doing?" Retta asked.

Shy Bear motioned for Retta to dig on the other end of the trench. Using sticks and their bare hands, they soon had a trench six inches wide, two feet long, and a foot deep.

Shy Bear tossed the shavings down in the hole. She reached into the pocket of her dress and pulled out a small, flat piece of rusted metal no bigger than a large coin. Holding it down in the trench, she struck it with what looked like a broken arrowhead. The result was a cascade of sparks, smoke, and then flames.

She stuck larger twigs on the fire. The flames licked up to the surface of the ground, where the wind acted as a barrier. With sticks and chips now burning, Retta put the large pot of water over the fire. The sides of the pot rested on the dirt edges of the slot-like fire pit.

"Thanks!" Retta said.

Shy Bear reached over and squeezed her hand. Then she stood and hiked back toward the river.

Mr. Barre stuck his head out of the wagon. "I thought I smelled a fire. Darlin', how did you do that?" he hollered above the dust storm.

Retta trotted over to the wagon. The canvas wagon top flapped and popped in the wind. "Shy Bear helped me, Papa."

"Darlin', grab that new pony of yours and ride out there and tell William to gallop across the river and see if he can find the wagon train. We need Mrs. Weaver back here right away. It looks like your mama is goin' to need extra help."

"Papa, I can go."

"Hurry, darlin'. There's no time to waste."

She heard her mother scream, "Eugene!" He popped back inside.

Lord, how can I hurry if I have to go find William in this dust storm? He didn't say for me not to go; he just said to hurry. Help me, Jesus.

Retta grabbed the rope reins and pulled herself onto the pinto's back. She galloped for the river. The eagle feather tickled her ear. Her buckskin dress pushed up above her knee-high moccasins. She leaned into the wind and hugged the horse's neck.

"Come on, boy . . . run . . . and run!"

Retta could only see a few dozen yards in front of the horse. The swirling dust stung her eyes. She passed Two Bears on the run and didn't attempt to wave. The pinto hit the river on the gallop and hardly slowed in the two-foot deep water. When they reached the south bank, she slammed her heels into his flanks. He galloped up the incline to the prairie.

By the time she reached the wagon trail, the wind was blowing so hard she could not see more than fifty feet. She stopped the horse and stared down at the dust swirling around the ruts of the trail.

"Oh dear, Muggins, I can't tell if they've reached this point or not. What do I do now?"

Lord, please tell me which way to go. I can't just stand here with dust in my eyes. They were two days ahead of us. Even with the shortcut, we can't have caught up already. They must be ahead of us.

Retta turned her horse straight into the stiff wind and kicked his flanks. He didn't budge.

"Come on, boy!" she yelled.

She kicked him again. He danced sideways but wouldn't move forward.

"Muggins, please! I know it's a bad wind, but we have to do this for Mama," she cried and kicked his flanks again.

Muggins jerked to the south.

"You can't turn tail." Her voice broke. She fought back the tears. "Mama needs us."

She kicked him as hard as she could. The paint horse broke into a gallop—straight east.

"No!" She tried to pull him back, but the horse would not slow his gallop. As she bounced along, barely able to hang on, the dust darkened around her. Retta could only see a few feet ahead. Without warning Muggins cut to the right. Retta grabbed the horse's mane with both hands.

A startled Bobcat Bouchet came into view and then disappeared in the dust.

"The wagon train! Muggins, we found it. You found it."

She reined up quickly and was on the ground next to the first wagon when Bouchet made it back to her.

"Missy, is that you?" he shouted through the wind.

Colonel Graves ran up to her side. "How on earth did you get ahead of us?"

"We took a shortcut. Mama's time has come, and she needs Mrs. Weaver. We're just across the river."

"Where's the river?" the colonel asked.

"About a mile north of here, I reckon. Please, I need to hurry."

"Hop on your pony. Let's go back to the Weaver wagon," the colonel instructed. He grabbed the rope halter and led the paint along the line of wagons.

A black-haired girl stuck her head out of the back of a wagon. "Retta, I never thought I'd see you again!"

"Joslyn! I've got to get Mrs. Weaver for Mama."

Joslyn jumped down and trotted beside Retta. "Is that your horse?"

"Yes, I told you I would get one!"

Ansley MacGregor rode up to her. "Retta! What're you doing here? Oh, I'm glad to see you. Where's your wagon?"

"On the other side of the river! I've got to get right back."

"I'll ride with you," Ansley offered.

When they reached the Weaver wagon, it was Ben who stood by the lead ox. "Retta!" he yelled.

She leaned over and shouted into the wind, "Is your mama in the wagon?"

"Yes!" Ben hollered. "The dust is so bad she went inside."

"I need her." Retta slipped down and trotted to the wagon.

Christen stuck her head out the back. "Retta!"

"I need your mother—quick! Mama's in bad shape across the river!"

Mrs. Weaver stuck her head out. "I'll get my things!" she shouted and then turned to Colonel Graves. "Get us a light wagon, colonel. I don't straddle a horse like these young girls!"

He scratched his head. "A light wagon? Oh . . . the new one!"

He led Retta and her friends down the parked line of wagons. They came up to a pair of mules and the paneled wagon. "Are they here?" she gasped.

The colonel stared at her. "You know them?"

Retta puffed out her cheeks.

"They're new. One of them got shot by Indians," Ben reported. "They barely escaped with their lives."

"Indians?" Retta folded her arms across her chest. "I shot him in the seat of the pants when he tried to steal our cows!"

"You what?" The colonel glanced over at Bobcat Bouchet and motioned for him to go to the back of the wagon.

"Colonel Graves," Retta declared, "they are horrible prairie pirates. Daddy said we should have shot them all."

The colonel banged on the side of the paneled wagon with his rifle butt. "Get out of there," he shouted.

Elmo stuck his head out and spied Retta in the dust. "What's she doin' here? That's the Injun who broke Davy's toes and shot him in the backside."

"Get out of the wagon," the colonel ordered, his rifle pointed at the man.

As Elmo climbed down, there was a commotion at the rear. Bobcat led Davy around to the front. "The other one objected, and I coldcocked him," Bouchet announced.

"She shot me! That Injun gal is the one that shot me!" Davy shouted as Bobcat shoved him along.

"She's no more Indian than I am," Bobcat fumed.

"But she's wearin' Indian garb!"

"And you're wearin' a gun, but that doesn't make you a gunman." The colonel pulled himself up into the wagon. "We're confiscating your wagon for a sick lady."

"You can't do that. It's got our personals," Elmo protested.

The colonel glanced inside the paneled wagon and then looked down at the two held at bay by Bobcat's gun. "Most everything in this wagon has been stolen from someone in this train."

"You want me to take them out on the prairie and shoot them?" Bobcat yelled out.

"You can't do that," Elmo hollered out.

"Of course we can," the colonel replied.

"Colonel," Retta called out, "there are army troops headed this way behind you. They should catch up with you soon."

"Good! Tie them up and leave them lying on the prairie."

He drove the wagon out of the line. "Now, Retta, I can't drive this wagon to your mother's because I have to be here to start up the wagon train as soon as the wind allows us to," he told her. "To be parked out in this dust storm would be dangerous for everyone."

"I'll drive it," Ben offered.

"I'll go with Ben," Joslyn called out.

By the time they picked up Mrs. Weaver, Joslyn, Ben, and Christen were also in the wagon. Retta, with Ansley MacGregor alongside her, led the wagon into the dust storm.

"How can you find where to cross the river?" Ansley shouted. Her red hair flagged out behind her, and her green eyes were almost squinted shut.

"I don't know," Retta called out. "The Lord will have to lead us."

"Or maybe an Indian girl?" Ansley shouted a reply.

Retta started to grin, but the sand got in her teeth. "No, I'm not that good at finding my way in a dust storm."

"I didn't mean you. I meant her!" Ansley pointed to the west.

In the shadows Retta spotted a familiar silhouette. "It's Shy Bear."

Retta galloped up to the girl, who straddled a buckskin horse. Without a word, she led them to the river.

When they arrived at the bank of the river, Two Bears was there. He jumped on the back of the lead mule that pulled the paneled wagon and guided the wagon across the river. They turned away from the wind and rolled along about a quarter of a mile. They were almost on top of the covered wagon before it came into view. Retta leaped off her horse as her father stuck his head out the front flap.

"I've got Mrs. Weaver, Papa! The wagon train is just across the river."

He pulled his bandanna up over his mouth to block the blowing sand and dirt.

"Thanks, darlin', but it's too late."

"What do you mean?" Retta shouted.

"It's too late," he hollered. "It's all over!"

Nine

"Over?" Retta was in tears. "How can it be over? I hurried as fast as I could, Papa."

"It's okay, darlin'," Mr. Barre assured her. "Mrs. Two Bears was very helpful."

Lerryn poked her head out. "She's beautiful!"

Retta puffed out her cheeks. "Mama?"

"No, silly." Lerryn grinned. "Jessica Laramie Barre!"

Retta could feel her heart race. "It's a girl?"

Lerryn nodded. "She's so tiny."

Retta spun around to the paneled wagon where Ben was helping Mrs. Weaver to the ground. "Did you hear that? It's a girl!" she hollered.

Christen and Joslyn clapped and then jumped down and ran over to her.

William climbed off the Barre wagon, his felt hat pulled down to his spectacles. Dust swirled around his face.

Retta grabbed her brother's arm. "What does she look like?"

"Mama?" he grinned.

Retta brushed sand out of the corners of her eyes. "No, what does little Jessica look like?"

Lerryn reached down her hand. "Come on, sis, but you better be prepared."

"Prepared for what?"

Andrew stepped alongside her and gave her a boost. "She's weeks early. She's very small and . . ."

"And what? What is it you won't tell me? Is something wrong?"

Lerryn took her hand and tugged her inside the wagon. "Oh, nothing's wrong with her. She just looks identical . . . to you!"

The evening was hectic. But the windstorm died down before dark, and so they crossed the river. The Barre wagon took the last position, behind old Sven Neilsen. And behind the Barres, Lucy Two Bears set up their camp.

Seated at the campfire next to the Barre wagon were Christen Weaver, Joslyn Jouppi, Ansley MacGregor, and a very pale Gilson O'Day. Retta stood at the side of the wagon, waiting for Lerryn to hand out a blanketed bundle. She walked slowly back to the girls, cradling the bundle in her arms.

Retta rocked the baby as she talked. "Here she is. This is my li'l sis, Jessica Laramie Barre."

The girls huddled around. Gilson remained seated on the trunk.

Retta stopped next to the short girl with curly brown hair. "Now, Jessie, this is Christen. She has been my friend ever since we were babies. She has stuck with me through everything. So if you find a friend like Christen, hang onto her. But never ask Christen about that boy camped out with his uncles down on Little Blue Creek."

"Retta!" Christen protested.

"What boy?" Ansley asked. "I don't remember a boy. How come I don't remember?"

Retta ignored the questions and stepped alongside the girl with the straight black hair. "Now this is Joslyn. I just met Joslyn when we started this trip, but she's a good friend already, and it seems like we've known each other forever. She's going to California to get rich. So when you grow up, she'll probably have one of the fine houses in San Francisco. She's very pretty, but she doesn't think she is. But the boys know. The boys always know who the pretty ones are. Jessie, I'll tell you all about girls like you and me later."

Retta pulled the blanket back from the baby's sleepy eyes and stepped up to the tallest girl. "Now, darlin', this is Ansley MacGregor. She used to be a real pill!"

"Retta," Christen cautioned.

"Oh, let her continue," Ansley laughed. "Retta's right, of course."

"But don't let her fool you," Retta continued. "Ansley is now a good friend, too. Ansley's problem is that she's too beautiful. All the girls are jealous, and all the boys act like monkeys around her."

Ansley continued to laugh.

"It's true." Retta turned to Joslyn and Christen. "It's true, isn't it?"

Both girls nodded their heads.

"But you and me, Jessie, don't have to worry about that." She sat down on the trunk. "Now, baby, this is Gilson. She's a very, very special friend. But Gilson has been kind of sick for a long time. She's the kindest, dearest girl I've ever met in my life. You and me are going to take care of her and make sure she gets to Oregon."

Retta saw a tear slip down Gilson's pale cheek.

"You want to hold her?" Retta asked.

"Oh, yes." Gilson's blue eyes shone. "May I?"

Gilson rocked the sleeping baby gently back and forth. "She's so beautiful."

"Well, I don't know about that. Lerryn says she looks just like me," Retta remarked.

"She does. She doesn't look like either your mama or papa," Christen added. "Just you."

"Lucky little girl," Retta said.

Gilson handed Jessica back.

"Sometimes I wonder if I'll live long enough to have a baby," Gilson murmured.

"Of course you will," Retta assured her.

"But you have to get married first," Christen laughed.

"I know that . . ." Gilson's voice was even more quiet than normal. "But it all seems so far away."

"I predict," Retta announced, "that ten years from now, every one of us will be a mama."

"I wonder which of us will be first?" Christen asked.

In unison Retta, Joslyn, Gilson, and Christen turned and looked at the red-headed girl.

"Why are you looking at me?" Ansley protested. Then she broke into a wide smile. "Okay . . . you're probably right. After all, I am the oldest."

"If I ever have a girl," Gilson said, "I'm going to name her Retta."

"No, you can't!" Christen objected. "I've been her friend forever. My oldest girl is going to be named Coretta Emily."

"What's her last name going to be?" Retta teased.

Christen clasped her arms together. "I don't know yet!"

"I wouldn't mind if my last name was Barre," Joslyn replied. "But then I couldn't name my daughter Coretta Emily Barre."

"I, for one, am not going to name my daughter Retta," Ansley said. "I was reading a book about San Francisco last night, and I came up with a wonderful name for a girl."

"What're you going to name her?" Retta asked.

"Victoria Evangeline DelMonte," Ansley declared.

Joslyn brushed her long hair behind her ears. "You're going to marry someone named DelMonte?"

"Yes, I am. I just decided that last night. I want a name that has a dramatic ring to it."

"Do you know anyone named DelMonte?" Christen pressed.

"Not yet," Ansley admitted.

"Retta," Lerryn called from the wagon. "Mama said Jessie needs to be back inside here."

Retta peeked at the closed eyes of the sleeping baby. "Well, li'l sis, that's big sis, and we have to do what she wants. But we'll stick together, you and me, 'cause we're both little sisters. And we look like each other!"

She had just reached the wagon when two boys ran up. One grabbed her shoulder. "Let us see the baby."

Retta turned around. "Oh, Jessica, look closely. These are what are called boys. You and me are girls. Boys are really quite smart and industrious and brave . . ."

Ben and Travis beamed.

" . . . until they get within twenty feet of a girl. Then they become really, really strange. But don't worry, I'll tell you all about that later." Retta grinned.

Ben leaned over the baby. "That's not true," he protested. "It's girls that are strange. Why . . . girls sit around and do nothin' but comb their hair for hours at a time. You never see boys do that."

Retta handed the baby back up to Lerryn. "That's very true, Jessie. I know some boys who never comb their hair at all."

Retta had just washed her face and was ready to crawl under the wagon into her bedroll when Two Bears walked up carrying a bundle under his arm.

"How is the little bear?" he asked.

"Oh, that's what I'll call her—'Little Barre.' She's very tiny and sleepy."

"Yes, and when she gets older, you will have to tell her about her other family," he said.

"She does look like me, doesn't she?"

Two Bears grinned. "She is still a little pale. She needs more prairie sun."

Retta laughed. "The Lord didn't give us all beautiful brown skin."

"I have noticed that. I wonder why?"

"I don't know." Retta shrugged.

"I believe I will ask Him someday."

"Are you going to heaven, Two Bears?"

"If your Jesus will take me. I want to see those Shoshone angels!" He grinned. "I have been reading *Pil-Grim's Pro-Gress*."

"Oh, yes, Jesus will take you!"

"Perhaps in the evenings between here and Fort Bridger, you can explain that book to me," Two Bears suggested.

"Oh yes . . . and you can teach me to speak Shoshone," Retta said.

He rubbed his hairless chin. "You would like to learn?"

"More than anything."

There was no smile on his face. "That could be dangerous."

"Why?" she questioned.

"We will soon be in Shoshone country."

"I know."

"And there will be many Shoshone warriors."

"Are they really dangerous?"

A grin sprang up on his face. "If you wear buckskins and speak Shoshone, they will all want to marry you!"

"Oh!" Retta frowned. "But I still want to learn Shoshone. Maybe the first thing I should learn to say is, 'I'm too young to get married.'"

"No, the first thing you should learn is a baby song."

"A baby song. You mean a lullaby?"

"Yes. Shy Bear can teach you one in Shoshone."

"That would be wonderful."

He handed her the bundle. "This is for you."

"What is it?"

"A baby present. Open it."

"Is it for Mama? I can take it to her."

"No, it is for Red Bear."

She unwrapped the antelope hide covering. "It's a beautiful cradle board!"

"My wife, Lucy, made it." Two Bears beamed.

"For Mama?"

"No, she made it for Red Bear. The day will come when your mother needs help with Little Bear. You can carry the baby on your back."

"And she'll get some sun."

"Then someday, when you are older, you can carry your own babies in the cradle board, and you will remember Two Bears and his family."

"Oh, thank you, Two Bears. You're such a good friend. You have helped me not to be afraid of Indians. At least, not all Indians."

"And you, Red Bear, have helped my family not to be afraid of white people. At least, not all white people."

The wind died. The air warmed at daylight. Laramie Peak beckoned in the west. The bugle sounded, and the wagons rolled and squeaked west on a dry, dusty trail.

Retta wore her brown cotton dress and high lace-up boots. A burlap sack hung over her shoulder. Joslyn paced on her right, Christen on her left. They both wore bonnets, but Retta was bare-headed.

"If we are almost to Fort Laramie, why do we still need more buffalo chips?" Christen complained.

Retta kicked at a clod. "Papa says we can never have too many."

"When I'm old, and my grandchildren ask me what it was like coming over the Oregon Trail, I'm going to tell them I spent five months gathering buffalo manure," Joslyn said.

"Not me," Christen declared.

Joslyn swatted two flies off her forehead. "What're you going to tell your grandkids?"

"I'm going to tell them I came across the trail with Retta Barre."

Retta rubbed her nose with the palm of her hand and then slapped a mosquito on her cheek. "And they'll say, 'Who?'"

Christen faked a grin. "But then I'll get to tell them all the Retta Barre stories."

"Like what?"

"Like the time she killed twelve charging buffalo with only a rock."

"What!" Retta exclaimed. "That's not true. There was one buffalo. He was already dead, and I had a coup stick."

"But you know how it is when you're old. You get things mixed up," Christen laughed.

"How about the time Retta got into a gunfight with a hundred prairie pirates?" Joslyn suggested.

Christen giggled. "Or the time she found the lost baby out in the prairie snow?"

"Wait a minute," Retta objected. "There's no snow in the summer."

"Okay." Christen shrugged. "A prairie dust storm."

Joslyn's hand flew up to her face. "And how about the time we caught her and Ben Weaver next to the river kissing!"

"You! You!" Retta puffed out her cheeks and held her breath. "You can't say that!" she protested. "It didn't even come close to happening!"

Christen raised her thin brown eyebrows. "The trip's not over yet, Coretta Emily Barre!"

The trio stopped and stared down at the dirt.

"Whose turn is it?" Joslyn asked.

"I guess it's mine," Christen replied. "Retta, would you mind?"

Retta scooped up the buffalo chip and jammed it into Christen's burlap sack.

The sun was straight above. The girls had emptied their sacks twice when they heard the shout. The long train of covered wagons pulled to a stop.

"I wonder what happened?" Joslyn muttered.

Christen wiped the sweat off her forehead with the sleeve of her green dress. "Someone probably broke an axle."

"I do hope there isn't a long wait," Retta mused. "Andrew said we might camp within view of Fort Laramie tonight. Won't it be grand? We haven't seen any building bigger than a dugout trading post in almost two months!"

Christen set her burlap sack on the dirt. "I'm going to buy a peppermint stick!"

"I need some material to sew a new dress." Joslyn tugged at the front of her dress. "This one is too tight, and I can't let it out anymore."

"Is she bragging again?" Retta teased.

In the distance they could see a horse gallop their way.

"Here comes Ansley," Joslyn observed.

Christen pulled off her bonnet and used it to wipe the dust off her neck. "Retta, how come you aren't riding Muggins?"

"'Cause I wanted to walk with you, and Papa said I had to pick up chips. Of course, I could ride along on my horse, and you two could pick up the chips and stuff them in *my* bag."

Both Christen and Joslyn stared at her and then rolled their eyes.

"That's what I thought! That's the reason I'm walking."

"Someone's riding with her," Joslyn called out.

"Is it Ben?" Retta asked.

"No," Christen answered, "it's Gilson!"

"Hi!" Retta greeted the two girls. "Where're you going in such a hurry?"

"To see you, of course," Ansley hollered as she approached.

Retta looked at the pale girl in the yellow bonnet that matched her blonde hair. "How're you feeling, Gilson?"

"Sick," Gilson said, "but I'd rather be riding and sick than lying in that wagon and sick."

"Why did you want to see me?" Retta queried.

"Why did the wagon train stop?" Christen asked.

"There's a bunch of Sioux warriors blocking the trail!" Ansley explained.

"Sioux? Oh, no! What did they want?" Retta gasped.

Ansley's horse pranced. She yanked back on the reins. "They want to talk."

"What about?" Retta asked.

"They won't say." Ansley leaned forward and patted her horse's neck. "They want to talk to Red Bear."

"Really? I—I don't know anything about the Sioux."

"The chief said he knew you."

"But—I don't . . . What's his name?"

"He calls himself 'Braces.'"

"Braces?"

"He wears leather suspenders holding up his buckskin trousers."

"Oh! That Indian!" she hollered. "I thought he was a Cheyenne. Ansley, you and Gilson go get Muggins and bring him here. Joslyn, help me put on my buckskin dress. Christen, find my headband, necklace, and coup stick."

"You mean your scepter?" Christen teased.

"Scepter?" Retta questioned.

"Coretta Emily Barre, you are the undisputed princess of this prairie."

Epilogue

Eugene Barre — Built a house and started a farm one hundred miles south of Oregon City, Oregon. D. August 1873.

Julia Barre — Continued in poor health. D. September 1873.

William Barre — Married Amy Lynch. Operated a farm and feed mill one hundred miles south of Oregon City, Oregon.

Andrew Barre — Operated a stage line, express company, and then a bank, just north of Oregon City, Oregon. He married Joslyn Jouppi in June 1859.

Lerryn Barre — Taught school in Oregon for fifty-seven years. In 1891 she wrote *Down the Trail with Retta Barre*. It is still considered the premier Oregon Trail narrative. She never married.

Jessica Laramie Barre — Married Tyler Carpenter in May 1874. He became an attorney and served twenty-three years on the Oregon Supreme Court.

Two Bears — D. in a hunting accident in the Big Horn Mountains at the age of ninety-one.

Shy Bear — D. of smallpox, February 1856

Christen Weaver — Married Travis Lott in July 1860. They lived on a farm one hundred miles south of Oregon City. Her eldest daughter was named Coretta Emily Lott.

Gilson O'Day — D. of tuberculosis, three days after arriving in Oregon. Her granite headstone is fenced in with black iron and is still maintained by Barre family descendants.

Joslyn Jouppi — Stayed three months in California and then migrated with an uncle to Oregon. She married Andrew Barre.

Ansley MacGregor — Married Lucky Nate DelMonte, who later made a fortune in the timber business in Washington Territory. Her mansion is now a museum overlooking the Columbia Gorge and can still be seen from Interstate 84. They had one daughter, Victoria Evangeline DelMonte.

Ben Weaver — Operated a farm one hundred miles south of Oregon City, Oregon, along the middle fork of the Willamette River. He married Coretta Emily Barre.

Retta Barre — Married Ben Weaver in July 1860. They farmed for over sixty years. She bore six daughters and one son. All but the son looked exactly like their mother.

For a list of other books
by this author
write:
Stephen Bly
Winchester, Idaho 83555
or check out his website:
www.blybooks.com